Life Seemed Good, But....

A collection of short quirky stories

By Richard J Bell

This book is dedicated to all those who have watched a loved one suffer from cancer, or any terrible illness. Writing it was my therapy.

Rated PG-13 for drug references, cartoon violence, bad puns and anti-humor.

TABLE OF CONTENTS

PROLOGUE

What's past is prologue, mostly.

MY PET SPUD

Some time ago I bought a sack of russet potatoes at the grocery store. When I found a lone tater hiding in my pantry several months later, I noticed it had developed eyes all over its body so I carefully plucked them out until there were two left. With these eyes perfectly formed and placed on this oblong, human-head shaped potato it gave the distinct impression that it was alive in the same sense you and I share that definition and experience. Fascinated, I stared at it for hours and sensed that it was aware of my presence.

I told the unemployment office I was looking for work in order to get my check, but I was totally preoccupied with this peculiar potato and the hold it had over me. After about two weeks, something quite extraordinary happened. The potato actually connected to my mind and spoke a word that sounded like "Fark." I swear this is true, and I wasn't on blue meth or anything.

I named him Spud.

Call me greedy, but it soon became apparent that one pet potato was not enough. Feeling the urge to have more, Spud and I went out and selected an additional dozen at the market. I drew a different face on each so I could tell them apart since they didn't yet have eyes, and wrote their names on the back of their heads. A week later, these new potatoes were thinking as well, thanks in part to Spud's influence.

Having thirteen intelligent potatoes was deemed to be unlucky and they convinced me to continue adding to their number. Then the question became, was there a way to refine the process to trigger each new potato's awareness more quickly and over greater distances?

Spud inspired me to fashion a hat of aluminum foil, put it on, and sit in a dark closet. While in there I hummed like a bee and concentrated on the Great Potato Spirit.

After twenty minutes, there was a sudden, brilliant flash of light in my mind, as though I had been contacted from another world. Upon leaving the closet I discovered I had gained mystical abilities limited only by my imagination.

Now we were able to liberate tubers by the hundreds simply by strolling through the produce section and giving them "the eye." I routinely visited the local food stores and occasionally traveled to supermarkets in nearby cities.

We agreed to give away the twelve as Ambassadors and Overseers to various store managers but keep Spud, whom I carry in a leather pouch hanging from my belt, for myself. As weeks went by, I pictured myself at the head of an enormous potato army thundering across the fruited plains. I was somebody special, all right.

Then one evening at dinner it struck me. I considered the fate of my potatoes and realized that each one was being eaten. Alive! They were being prepared and cooked, with their consciousness intact, in all sorts of horrible ways. Instead of being their grand liberator, I had become a villain, condemning thousands of innocent potatoes to a conscious awareness of their own deaths…all except the first potato. I could never eat him.

But now, Spud has turned and become my tormentor and a constant reminder of the unimaginable evil I have done. Every day begins with, "Good morning. Fark, I hate you," and then he starts telling me what a bad person I am and dredging up things from my past. Despite trying to reason with him, he refuses to accept any responsibility for what we did together.

What's more, I suspect that mushrooms have been watching me. They're sneaky little things; they think I don't notice, but I do!

I am now going to lock myself in the cellar until this whole thing blows over. If you'd like to join me, I'll tell you a few stories I know.

EAT ME

Not so long ago there was a friendly herd of caterpillars that lived in the Mystee forest, in a comfy little glen that had all the food, water, and shelter they needed to be happy. Every morning it took them an hour to put their shoes on and in the evening, an hour to remove them. Tradition required shoes.

Each caterpillar bore the same markings on their backs, which they were born with. Being like furry, colorful sweaters, if a bird or small animal looked at the pattern, it read "Eat me, I am so delicious." The caterpillars did not realize this and believed the design meant "I am fun to be with." Their existence was, for the most part, very pleasant.

Among the herd were two young caterpillars named Kenny and Kyle who were best friends. They were also the fastest runners and had special shoes that were custom made from the finest grass clippings and spider silk. Everywhere they went they ran as rapidly as possible and were always first in line for bingo, shuffleboard, and when the wading pool was opened. They also liked running circles around the slugs, laughing and calling them names like "asstropod" (instead of gastropod). Overall, they were good young caterpillars who were respectful of adults.

One afternoon, as they were resting in the shade of a dogwood tree, a snapping turtle whizzed by at lightning speed (comparatively) and left them in the dust. Our two caterpillars were impressed.

"Wow!" Kenny cried. "Did you see that?"

"Barely," Kyle replied. "If it comes back, let's jump on and go for a ride." So they climbed up a very short tree and out onto a low hanging branch, hung on by their fingertips, and waited. After what seemed like hours but was only three minutes, the turtle returned from where it had been. The courageous caterpillars let go as it passed underneath and they bounced and rolled but hung on for dear life. The two climbed to the top of the turtle's shell and before they knew it they were speeding like mad across the field.

"This is amazing!" Kenny cried. "I'm having trouble breathing, we're going so fast."

"I'm freaking out," Kyle replied. "Now how in the world do we get off?" The turtle continued at breakneck speed and the caterpillars were terrified. They shouted for it to stop but the turtle didn't hear them, so to get its attention they threw their tiny shoes at its head.

That didn't work either. Their mad joy ride continued unabated until they despaired of life itself. Eight minutes later, they all came to a grinding halt beside a peaceful stream, and the caterpillars had no idea where they were.

"This is all your fault, fuzz-brain!" Kenny cried.

"You were the one who agreed to it," Kyle replied.

"What are we, nuts?" they both said simultaneously. Kenny and Kyle continued to argue and then spent time angrily throwing their remaining shoes at each other.

Soon they realized how foolish they were being and slid off behind the turtle, which then waddled into the stream. The two caterpillars, now without shoes, were amazed at how good it felt to feel the pure ground beneath their feet. They must tell the other caterpillars of this life-changing discovery! They glanced up at the sun to get their bearings and, using a rudimentary internal magnetic compass, began the long trek toward home.

Meanwhile, high above on a branch, an owl was reading the backs of their sweaters.

AMOEBA LIPS

Frankie was an ordinary, nearsighted amoeba living in his tiny world, wherever that was, it doesn't matter. He was pretty much indistinguishable from the others but there was one distinct trait that set him apart, which was this: he loved kissing all the girl amoebae...and Frankie believed almost every other amoeba was a girl. Often he would hide and wait for one to come by then leap out like a playful puppy and plant a big kiss on whichever part of their body that was facing him.

One day he kissed Grouchy Bob on his left kneecap. Grouchy Bob yelled and shamed him, but it went in one ear, through his nucleus, and out the other ear with no discernable effect.

As he stood there feeling somewhat perplexed, his goofy friend Jay came by and asked him, "Who was that big zygote I observed you with last night?"

"That was no zygote," quipped Frankie, "that was a paramecium!"

"You dated the Mecium twins?" Jay asked jokingly. They both laughed like crazy then Jay sped away and Frankie went in search of more girl amoebae.

Eventually, Frankie got a bad reputation and when another of his kind saw him coming, it would contract its pseudopods and locomote in the opposite direction as fast as it could go. After a few days of this, Frankie got discouraged. Meeting Grouchy Bob again he asked, "Gee, what's the problem? Don't you girls like being kissed?"

Bob put an intelligent look on its face and stated, "Let me explain something to you, Frankie. We are one-celled organisms and we reproduce by dividing down the middle. There's a word for it, I forget what it is. Therefore, there *are* no girl amoebae and you have been putting your big, slimy amoeba lips on anyone and everyone, and we're sick and tired of it. Last week you kissed old Jackson on the butt, and it's still upset. Everyone is laughing at you behind your cytoplasm, you know."

Frankie gazed at the ground with tears welling up, feeling like a big idiot. Why hadn't anyone told him this earlier? All the joy of life drained from him and he was so upset that he shook like jello. It would be difficult to apologize to everyone as they would all laugh him to scorn, so amidst the withered waste of his life he wandered away.

Several days later, he came upon a new colony of amoebae. The lesson he learned had completely vanished from his tiny mind and all he cared about was kissing girl amoebae. He pursued them and kissed them all, causing quite a commotion.

"Who is this immature amoeba?" they wondered.

It wasn't long before one of them, named Bob (by coincidence), confronted Frankie and explained the facts of life to him (again).

"Listen to me, you little diploid!" Bob fumed in closing, "You keep your damn amoeba lips to yourself. Do you hear me? Look at me when I'm talking to you!"

Two days later, Frankie subdivided and spent the next ten minutes kissing his twin until it was strong enough to get away.

Some people never learn.

SPUD'S REVENGE

I used to have a pet potato named Spud who didn't like me much; he told me so repeatedly. Anyway, he became old and wrinkly so despite his protests I gave him a burial in my backyard, six feet deep. I presumed that was the end of him. However, it appears that during the winter and following spring, old Spud kept growing, extending his roots and transforming into a huge mutant potato.

I first noticed something was odd when I dreamed of potatoes night after night. In the beginning they were happy little taters, but after two months turned angry and a bit frightening. I sought professional help but the doctor just kept asking about my mother. Following that, he put me on antidepressant drugs which made me feel like a human marshmallow and caused me to become more emotional and feel all clammy inside. So I stopped taking them.

But, as I soon realized, Spud had gained the ability to influence my thoughts and actions. For instance, I was forbidden to mow the lawn. I had to fertilize and water him for hours at a time which made me lose my job and have to beg money from family and friends. I was also instructed to address him as "King Potato-Pants."

He informed me that his ultimate goal was world domination with a plan to form a ruling class of potatoes like himself to enslave us before our final extermination. King Potato-Pants would see to it that no one on Earth ever ate another potato. His plot involved forcing spud farmers to instead plant hemp, which he seemed overly fond of. Additionally, he was going to restrict the use of butter, sour cream, and chives.

In order for him to learn more about humans, I was required to install a widescreen TV on the side of the house which he watched constantly with inquisitive eyes poking up through the ground. Daytime talk shows were his favorites.

This potato gradually grew so big that it formed a small hill in my yard. Then one summer morning, to my dismay, he lifted himself free of the ground and walked unsteadily on his giant root feet. A large eye with a laser death-beam emerged from the top of his head, and it reminded me of the H.G. Wells story *War of the Worlds*, with King Potato-Pants as the creature from Mars. I tried to call 911 but he punished every hint of rebellion with severe headaches followed by the irrational urge to move to Alaska.

King Potato-Pants began roaming around, destroying buildings and parking lots to create open fields to grow more mutant taters. Flames and smoke followed his path of destruction through several counties. No one dared get close enough to read him his rights or thump him to see how ripe he was. Even the military became helpless when his mind-web extended through the Internet. It was the beginning of the rout of civilization, of the massacre of mankind.

Two weeks later, as King Potato-Pants was clomping through Waukegan, Illinois, he suddenly stopped in his tracks, wobbled a bit, and fell to the ground with a sickening "thunk."

The King was dead!

Somehow he was destroyed from within, possibly by germs or pollution or potato bugs. Scientists came and took samples but nothing was ever revealed. Personally, I think he was slowly poisoned by television, from which his mind had no natural immunity.

He was subsequently cut up and made into chips and fries and sold to distribution centers all across the country.

Unfortunately, Spud got his final revenge. Everyone who ate of him turned into a permanent couch potato with an overwhelming appetite for daytime talk shows.

CASINO

Oscar felt great; better than he ever had his entire life. He was rolling dice at the craps table in his favorite casino, hitting all the numbers and "raking in the lettuce." Lady Luck was in the dice and she knew his name. Oscar had a free chocolate martini and three dozen admirers watching him roll, and the chips were coming like flies to a cow pie. Late into the night and early morning he played and eventually the worried pit boss made a phone call.

Soon the manager and all the security personnel were observing him through the video monitors, looking for signs of cheating. Another pit boss stood ten feet from the lucky guy and stared at him through binoculars. Oscar was betting higher and higher amounts and still winning. At this rate, management became concerned that he would win more than they could pay. Asking him to leave or staging a fire drill were considered, but he was legally entitled to be there and the odds did favor the house. Oscar felt the urge to bet it all and rolled one more time to break the bank.

"Yeah, baby," Oscar exclaimed, "I'm rich!" And already he was spending it. He ordered a beer and a grilled cheese sandwich for himself and everybody in the casino. Of course, for that many sandwiches they had to be put on back-order and lots of patrons never got theirs.

The owner and CEO, Mr. Aristotle, walked over and asked to have a word with him.

"Truth is you've won quite a lot here. Changing the dice a dozen times did not affect you one iota," he mused, pacing back and forth while rubbing his chin hair. Mr. Aristotle told him to hang tight while they figured things out.

This had never occurred before, and management was not sure what to do. Should they give him the keys to the casino, sign over rights, and make him the new owner?

They hurriedly called a meeting and, in the meantime, comped Oscar the best room in the hotel and sent up a bottle of champagne. After a frenzied consultation, the lawyers came up with a desperate plan of action.

While Oscar was sleeping, a bellboy snuck into his room, planted a small bag of marijuana in his coat pocket, and tied a she-goat to the bed frame. Early in the morning, while he was still passed out, the police, acting on a tip, came in with a search warrant and photographers.

At the trial, Oscar was accused of corrupting the morals of a quadruped, but was only found guilty of possession of an illegal, green, leafy substance. All his winnings were returned to the casino because the judge ruled that playing while high had given him an unfair advantage. The old goat claimed she had been set up and framed and it was all a ba-a-a-ad misunderstanding.

The owner and the manager celebrated by dancing the hokey-pokey on their desktops, putting their whole selves into it. Poor Oscar spent a week in the slammer, and, in exchange for his freedom, was ordered to pay a huge fine. He was then escorted to the airport by the local police and rudely ordered to never return.

No one ever guessed that tiny extraterrestrials, aliens that resemble fleas, were responsible for the entire episode. They manipulated the dice using mini-force fields and put various urges into people's minds to control their behavior. Since the aliens are so small, it makes them feel bigger and more important to mess around with humans, plus they think it's extremely hilarious. In fact, I believe one of them may be putting an idea into your head at this very moment.

So now what do you think?

Don't be so sure.

THE LEGEND OF TIMMY
(A CHILDREN'S STORY)

Hi kids. Let me tell you about a pack of porcupines that lived in the dark, scary part of the Mystee forest. They had fairly decent living conditions but there was a mean herd of skunks that had moved in nearby, who would take food, toys, and furniture away from the poor porcs and cause a big stink if they didn't get their way. This annoyed the porcupines and they got sick and tired of it after a couple of months.

One day, the porcupine named Timmy went berserk and took a chainsaw and chopped all the skunks to pieces. (Don't *you* ever try this.) It was like a horrible nightmare and in the process the skunks all sprayed him, causing a permanent stench that would never ever wash away.

Timmy had sacrificed himself for the pack and was allowed to stay in the vicinity only if he promised to stay downwind. The others were grateful, make no mistake, but stinky is stinky and we must not let anything unpleasant interfere with our enjoyment of life, right? He, of course, cared passionately for his fellow porcupines and was sad and perplexed as he went home, packed up his stuff, and plodded out to the perimeter.

Four months later, a herd of kangaroos moved in. They took over where the skunks had lived and threw their weight around like they owned the place. The kangaroos displayed the annoying trait of "hopping about" which worried the porcupines and made some of them dizzy, and they wondered what could be done.

After a heated discussion they sent for smelly Timmy and asked if he could do something to help as he had previously - a personal sacrifice of some sort. Timmy considered things carefully and got his hopes up that they would let him return if he did well. He always considered himself a type of healer in the community despite his tendency toward mindless violence.

Late that evening, Timmy and his unpleasant smell went into the camp of the kangaroos and raced around stabbing them with his sharp quills. They hopped and stomped but Timmy was too fast for them to catch, and the 'roos all got punctured and ran away. By this time Timmy was out of quills, so now he was smelly and bald. He went back to the porcupines and they were grateful, but would not let him return because of the way he looked and smelled. Timmy wept silently as he slowly walked back to the border.

A couple of months later, a crowd of wild mutated cantaloupes moved in and started to take over the place (um, they were very threatening cantaloupes, trust me). Just as before, the porcupines called on Timmy. He went in that very night and running faster than ever, took big bites out of each one of those fruits, causing severe damage. All the while he again hoped for redemption.

After successfully ridding his friends of this new menace, Timmy went to see what they would say. Now he was smelly, bald, and chunky. The porcupines remained adamant that he not return and Timmy became angry with them. When it was time to leave, instead of walking away dejected, he snarled and returned to the house he used to live in and stayed there. The porcs realized they could do nothing about it and had to resign themselves to his unpleasant presence.

They did not know a time was coming when they would need him again in that dark, scary part of the Mystee forest.

And so, children, this is how the legend of Timmy the smelly, bald, fat porcupine began.

THE PSYCHIC

I used to drive daily past a rundown storefront that advertised "Psychic and Mind Reader." As I passed, I would often mentally scream (Aaaaaaarggghhh!) over and over and crack up laughing. If she was real, I'm sure that annoyed her something fierce and she probably curled into a little ball as I drove by and cried, "I'm-a gonna find dat guy and make 'im stop, I tells ya dat!" I've encouraged my friends to do this routine but no one takes me seriously (except my mom...maybe).

On alternate days I mentally screamed using different tones of voice, sometimes with a foreign accent, so she would think it was different people. I'd also repeat crazy thoughts for her like, "Tonight I shall eat the entire supply of blue yogurt from the planet Vormfordooz" and "I woke up the Giant Turtle King. Run for your life!" Generally the messages were bizarre and amusing (to me at least) and designed to convince her she was going insane and maybe should find another line of work. Psychics are all fakes anyway, I think.

So, it was kind of a surprise that while driving by one day and sending her mental images of farting horses, I saw her come running out the front door dressed like a dime store gypsy and shaking her fist at the traffic. I was having real fun now.

One time, on my way home, I started the mental screaming from a mile away and continued as I approached. And there she was at the curb with her hands cupping her ears, staring directly at me. I had been identified! She probably knew my name and address via telepathy so there was no escape. I made a quick decision and pulled over to get the confrontation done with.

She came running up to my parked car, banged on the roof with her tiny fists and yelled, "Whatcha doin' yellin' like dis? You crazy? Why you keep screamin' at me every time you drive by here, I ask you dat!?" I rolled down the window.

"Look, I'm sorry, ma'am. I didn't realize you heard me," I lied. "Plus it was kind of funny, you have to admit." I gave her a nice big smile.

"You tink dats funny?" she shrieked, "I give you funny!" And she reached into my mind with whatever ESP she had and made me exit my car and bunny-hop down the street with my pants around my ankles. After a minute she stopped, figuring she had taught me a lesson, and I drove home humiliated.

But I wasn't about to let her win that easily. The following day I found my aluminum foil hat and brought it with me. After I had passed the storefront, I took it off and mentally screamed louder than ever and added a few suggestions not intended for the general public. In my rear-view mirror I saw her tattered curtains fly open and knew she would be waiting for me when I returned.

Sure enough, as I drove back that evening, she was by the curb with her family, all intent on making me stop and do who-knows-what shameful act. I quickly put on the foil hat and laughed as I drove by, waving at her. She appeared furious and I assumed I was safe because, after all, I had kept driving.

However, when I arrived at my humble abode, my cat went psycho and attacked, clawing me all over.

I learned my lesson and quit annoying her. Besides, have you ever tried to make a cat wear aluminum foil on its head?

GRILLED CHEESE

Not long ago, there was a grilled cheese sandwich that came suddenly into conscious existence as the result of an order at a cafeteria combined with a mysterious miracle. His bread was toasty brown and his cheese nicely melted. He felt satisfied with being a grilled cheese sandwich and life seemed good. All around him were clean, shiny aluminum surfaces and cabinets. There was also an aroma he couldn't quite place. It smelled kind of like cheese and he wondered if he had farted without knowing it.

He was sitting there a while, trying to count his toes, when a spatula came and lifted him up. As he was removed from the grill he noticed an older woman staring at him intently, and he heard the cook tell her that her sandwich was almost ready. Was he the sandwich being spoken of? He assumed so and hoped she would be nice to him.

Shortly thereafter, he found himself plopped onto a Styrofoam plate so he sat there contentedly, waiting to see what might happen next. He was joined by a ripe green pickle which he believed would be his lifelong friend and companion. A minute later, some extremely hot French fries jostled into him and he felt like he had a real family now. The plate was then handed to the lady who took him away from the only home he had ever known.

She brought him and his traveling companions into the cool air of the dining area. He looked around with astonishment at this new and dazzling world, but then had a disturbing vision of other grilled cheese sandwiches that appeared to be in different stages of being "all there." Setting the tray on a table she sat, picked him up, and blew on him for a while, which tickled. Then she slowly brought him to her lips, which were opening wider as he approached. All at once it dawned on him what was happening.

"Stop, don't do this," he shouted in panic, "I have my rights. You put me down this instant!" He called out to the fries for help, but they were frozen with terror. There was no escape, and how unfair it all was.

"Who knows," he contemplated sadly, "I might have grown up to become a club sandwich, or maybe even a cheeseburger."

Desperately he screamed, "I am Grilled Cheese Sandwich and I want to live!" while glaring at her. All she noticed was the chatter of the cafeteria.

He watched his brief life flash before his eyes and then she took a bite out of him and chewed. It did not hurt like he expected it to. In fact, he felt nothing at all. He seemed to be as intact as when he left the grill. The fries went bravely to their fate, not a whimper from any of them, and the pickle sat there, ignored and oblivious to it all.

When the lady came to her last bite of Mr. Sandwich, he found himself floating in space without a body and saw a bright light approaching, which he gazed at peacefully.

The light turned out to be the light above the grill in the cooking area, and he realized he had come back as another grilled cheese sandwich.

Fate can be a cruel joker.

THE WIZARD

It was midnight, and in the cold shadows of the murky forest the dark wizard sat on his gray horse and surveyed the sleepy little village before him. With the chilly wind at his back he rode slowly forward, his hand on the haft of his sword and his senses heightened. Danger lurked nearby.

Darkened windows and an eerie silence gave evidence to suppose that everyone was asleep. Unexpectedly, his horse came to a halt, refusing to take another step despite the urging of the Gothic-looking rider. He dismounted and gazed around warily. Without warning, his horse passed gas loudly and bolted down the road with most of his supplies. The wizard cursed menacingly under his breath.

He walked along until his shadowy shape came to a dimly lit inn next to the cobblestone road. Stopping to listen at the door, he heard not a sound.

"The peasants must be slumbering," he mused, "for if they knew who I was...standing at their door...they would be cringing in terror!" He moved onward.

As he walked he recalled the events in life that had brought him thus far: his birth in Russia to the Rostov family and the many train rides across Europe with his father. After that came his arrival at Wizard (pronounced wee-zerrrd) School. Leaving his family had filled him with great sorrow.

He took his final exam three times, and he failed three times. He remembered getting angry and challenging a powerful wizard to a duel, and losing. As a result, he had had the Maladroit Spell cast on him and was locked in a high tower, in his underwear, for punishment. Then there was a desperate escape and pursuit, followed by petty squabbling with his smelly horse as they crossed the Atlantic as stowaways. Upon being discovered, the pair jumped ship and swam ashore on the eastern coast of the Mystee forest.

The crescent moon was rising higher in the east now. Striding between the trees, he inadvertently tripped on a root, fell, and skinned his knee. The wizard clenched his teeth in fierce determination and limped on. Coming to a swiftly running brook, the mysterious foreigner knelt down to drink, whereupon he slipped and put his boot in the water up to his knee. He withdrew it cursing under his breath and poured out the water. A place to shelter and hide for the daylight hours would be needed before long.

An hour later, still following the rustic trail, he heard birds begin warbling the approach of dawn. He crept into the deep, dark woods and set up his wooly brown robe as a tent. Crouching inside, he ate his frugal meal of potato borscht, and something went down the wrong pipe. The wizard coughed for several minutes which gave him the hiccups and, you guessed it, he cursed under his breath.

As he prepared to retire he reflected on whether or not his quest was somehow connected to a grail (pronounced grrrail). He could not recall but felt the urge to keep traveling westward. The wizard looked at the emptiness inside himself and recollected the words of the sage who said, "Pure and complete sorrow is as impossible as pure and complete joy." He reflected on this as the sun peeked over the distant hills, and then closed his eyes.

While the secretive stranger dozed uneasily, a porcupine named Timmy (who was cursing under his breath) arrived and chewed through the rope supporting the tent, causing it to fall and spurring the dark wizard to search for another place to camp. As the gnarled figure skulked away he threw a spell at our four-legged hero, which caused the porcupine to imagine he had recently completed medical school, with predictably hilarious results.

And so, the Legend of Timmy the smelly, bald, fat, foul-mouthed porcupine continues.

TIME TRAVEL

I have ofttimes considered the possibility of time travel. I've also seen a few of those movies and decided to give it a try. It took longer to make the time machine than I expected, which may be ironic if I think about it long enough. It consisted of a big cardboard box with a round, cellophane window, lots of aluminum foil, a green laser, and four intricately wired electric guitar effects pedals attached to the gears of a grandfather clock. I finished building it just in time…. That's a time joke. Never mind.

But now, where could I go, and with what purpose? This needed to be considered carefully because changing the past can change the present, and seeing the future can alter *it* as well. I had to choose something quite simple to start with, so my first trip would be back a thousand years from my front yard.

Sitting in the box, I switched on the machine and observed with wonder the images that flickered before my eyes. After a minute, I arrived at a forested area with a lake roughly one hundred yards to the west. There were birds chirping and I watched the squirrels and rabbits that frolicked nearby. I sat there and threw dirt clods at them to make them move faster so I'd have some entertainment.

After an hour of that I became bored, so I returned to the present and researched my area at the library to see what happened in the past that might be interesting. That was a complete waste of time since I couldn't find anything remotely interesting. The next day, I went back fifteen hundred years and sat in the same forest for an hour. That's when I realized time travel was not what I expected. Heck, I could drive to a forest preserve for a similar experience and not smell like aluminum foil when I returned home.

A week later, I turned the machine on and traveled forward in time for a thousand years. What strange developments of humanity, what wonderful advances upon our civilization, I thought, might not appear when I came to look into the dim elusive world that raced and fluctuated before my eyes? When I stopped I was seemingly in the same forest but my house and the lake were gone.

I chose to initiate contact with someone from the future instead of the past because I don't want to accidentally change the present; I kind of like it at times. I searched around calling to see who might answer, hoping there weren't any Morlocks nearby. I didn't find anyone at first, but then I heard a distant voice.

Every time I yelled, "Hello," I heard a voice respond with a complimentary "Hello!"

I called "Who's there?" and the fellow replied "Who's there?" I ran in the direction of the sound, and it wasn't long before I did meet someone. It was me!

This was certainly unprecedented. We sat together and I learned that I was doing the same thing "I" was doing, but from a different starting point in the past. He told me a few jokes but I already knew the punch lines, and it was oddly reassuring to talk to someone who was exactly on my wavelength.

We wondered, "What might be better than this? Even more of me! If two could make it, why not three? Why not ten? Was there a limit?"

Now I'm thinking that I should get a bunch of my kindred selves together for a party. I and I are not sure how to arrange it, but if every time I read this story I travel forward to that same place in time, soon there will be a large gathering of me there. Hey, and remember to bring your own beer.

Added later - Everybody brings their own chair.
Added later - Bring a flashlight, I can't find my shoe.
Added later - The party is over, you drunken perverts!

THE SHOE

Once there was a family of poor immigrants who lived in the bayou part of the Mystee forest way back in 1954. They were so destitute that they couldn't even afford dirt to be dirt-poor. They had traveled all the way from a land called Hoboken and had picked this location by throwing a dart at a big map. These were simple, ordinary people who wanted the freedom to live any way they chose, within reason of course.

They arrived in the bayou and bartered for a crappy piece of real estate on a lake in the middle of nowhere. Their house was on stilts so that during the wet season it wouldn't totally fill with water. As they settled in, folks in the area helped them get adjusted and they learned to fish and grow pickles for a living. The locals were friendly but their dialect was hard to understand at first. Nevertheless, Paw was able to join a Cajun band playing the triangle and life was good. They had food, lots of water, and a roof over their heads but things are seldom as they appear.

Ruben, who was a bit "speshul," was the youngest of the family and he liked sitting on the porch whittling, watching the sun sparkle like diamonds on the water, and marveling at the stuff that drifted by. It was he who discovered the shoe and fetched it up as it was floating along. Ruben poured out the water and spoke to it like it was alive. He had been taught that every shoe had a soul, so he named it Terry. (Spelling was not one of his strengths.)

"Bonjou, old shoe. Whatcha doin' here? You smell bad-bad." The shoe said nothing.

"Can I tells you somethun funny, Terry? I wish I was a bird so I could fly far, far away from here. Or maybe I could be a dragonfly. Did you know a dragonfly can sting you seventeen times all at once? Talk to me, shoe. Don't just stare at me like that. I needs help to grow up so I can stop being pinned down by the thoughts of others and get away from here. I also needs me some new underwear, ya hear me? Terry?"

He confided to it quietly for several minutes with no response, so he called his father, "Hey Paw, come see whut I gots. Paw.... Hey, Paw, come take a look at this. Paw!"

The father staggered out a few moments later, shielding his eyes from the sun and demanding, "Oy, what's with the shoe? For this my nap you interrupt?"

The boy replied, "Look at it, Paw, it don't answer me none when I talk to it." The father gazed out on the waterfront, lost in contemplation. The old country was so far away. Now memories of life in the tenement flooded his awareness: the screaming children, the pervasive smell of garlic, and the shoe that had come sailing out of nowhere and hit him in the head. What was this, an omen? Of what?!

He noticed his son cradling the soggy shoe and said, "You there. Ruben. Hey, Ruben...hand me that shoe. Hey son, I'm talking to ya, hand me that thing," and the boy handed it up to him, still wet and slimy. The father peered inside and sure enough, the shoelace was wrapped tightly around the tongue of the shoe.

"No wonder it can't talk, boy, its tongue is tied. And it smells bad-bad," he said, and threw Terry as far as he could across the lake. Then he playfully smacked his son on the back of his head as together they watched it bob up and down. A moment later, a big catfish nibbled at it and the shoe sank out of sight.

"Damn," mumbled the shoe, "so close and yet so far. I coulda had class. I coulda been a contender. I coulda been somebody instead of a bum taking a dive."

INCIDENT AT THE DINER

There was a horse not so long ago that had the nickname of Farty-Horse. He had a shiny, dapple gray coat, eyes like blackest coal, and hooves that sounded like thunder when he ran. He also had an embarrassing problem he couldn't control. This stallion was a troublemaker and a stinker, not the sort who took kindly to being ridden. In fact, he disliked humans as much as he disliked the local Goth ferret population. (It stems from when he was a weanling and he and his mom had been frightened one day by a giant, ferret-shaped hot-air balloon. Fearing the daylight hours, mom became a night mare to live with.)

One afternoon, Farty-Horse felt bored and decided to start some trouble at the local ferret hangout called the Road Kill Diner and teach them a lesson about respect, but first, a nap. He set his alarm for 6:00 p.m. and lay down. When the alarm rang he was still tired, so he turned it off and rolled over for another forty winks. His girlfriend, Missy, knew he wanted to get up so she poked him a few times, but that had no effect; he mumbled and rolled over.

She yelled, "Hi Ho, Silver, away!" in his ear but he snorted and ignored it. Lastly, she got a bucket of cold water and threw it on him, but that only made him fart. Missy gave up and slammed the door as she left the room. Meanwhile, the horse was dreaming he was at the diner stomping ferret butts, and what fun he was having!

As he was leaving the diner in his dream, he saw a dark shadow in the distance that was rapidly approaching. He froze in fear as he realized it was a giant, floating ferret with flames intermittently shooting out of its bottom. He had no idea what was happening and cried out for mercy. Mr. Horse heard his girlfriend's voice come from it, telling him what a loser he was. Then he felt that feeling in the pit of his stomach like he was falling and Farty farted offensively and awoke with a great shock.

With his nerves almost completely shot he went to the diner, ordered eight beers, and drank them all at once. He sat there in a depressed mood, staring at the darkness through the open window. The Goth ferrets were watching him nervously, and two minutes later one of them, named Barnabas, valiantly ran over and bit him on the ankle. This greatly surprised the horse and made him fart and run out of the place in embarrassment.

Suddenly feeling fearless, all the ferrets followed. They jumped him, held him down, and colored his hooves and eyelids black and braided his tail. Following that, they forced him to swallow pebble-sized pieces of raw copper and zinc, telling him they were happy-pills. One of them made terrible puns as this was occurring and Farty had his feelings offended.

When they let him up, Fart noticed change coming from within. His anger was boiling over and he wanted to get away from everybody and start a new life somewhere else, so he screamed, "I hate you all, you freaky little idiots!" and bolted. Faster and faster he galloped, sounding like thunder. He felt another fart forming; it was going to be a big one, and he held it in. Unfortunately, the metal clanging around his innards caused a tiny spark that ignited the gas inside him, causing a huge explosion.

BOOM!

Rest in peace, Mr. Horse (whose real name was Melvin).

That's all, folks.

And let that be a lesson to any brassy critics. Don't expect Farty-Horse to make cents.

Commentary: To be clear, copper and zinc are used for coinage.

KILLING SOME TIME

Everyone uses the expression "killing some time," but I don't think anyone has ever literally tried to murder time. One day last April the idea struck me as a way to have a little fun so I decided to actually try to kill time. I do things like that.

I first had to find the time to kill time. Well, my afternoons were pretty much free since I was between temp jobs. Ten minutes might be enough but I wasn't sure how long it takes time to expire. I went out for a smoke and it wasn't long before a brilliant plan dawned on me. I'd create a trap, wait until the time was right, and spring the ambush before time could run out. I planned to kill the time between 4:20 and 4:30 p.m. and I'd use my cell phone (placed on my porch by the side door) for bait to ensure that time was really present.

Lastly, I needed a weapon. What is time's natural enemy? Is it freezing atoms to absolute zero or traveling at or above the speed of light? A lot of people kill time by doing something but, like I said, I wanted to go further than that. I intended to murder time, and, as far as I know, that's not against the law…yet. Since time is tricky and hard to pin down, my plan called for a weapon that would cover a large area. I filled a spray bottle with gasoline, added a few drops of thyme oil, and got a book of matches. I was convinced that burning time would kill it, at least ten minutes of it, in my little area. To protect myself from any weird supernatural events I'd wear my aluminum foil hat.

One has to be scientific to do these things properly.

Climbing up onto the roof with my supplies, I was ready. I was going to kill time like never before and was prepared to live with the consequences, whatever they might be. I had another smoke to pass the time. Waiting nervously, I experienced a myriad of primordial emotions and deep, puzzling doubts that I could bore you with by sharing, but why bother...nobody cares. I was all alone on the roof and, metaphorically, in the world...sigh....

After what felt like hours, I looked down at my cell phone and saw time reach 4:20 p.m. so I knew it was high time to begin. I put on my foil hat and sprayed gasoline at the unsuspecting time that floated there, innocently minding its own business. When it was soaked pretty good, I lit and tossed matches. Soon the phone and all the time around it were on fire. The heat was intense.

Some moments later I heard odd crackling noises so I knew I had done it; the invisible time was dying in the flames. I had burned that time to a crisp and I laughed at it, fiendishly almost. However, part of me was sad that I had killed innocent time for no good reason other than my own selfish entertainment. (I still wonder about that.) But anyway, now for a big victory celebration and ice cream and potato chips and whatever else I have lying around.

Coming down the ladder, I noticed my porch was on fire. That wasn't good, so I ran to get the hose but the water was still turned off inside from over the winter. I couldn't get in to turn it on because the front door was locked and the side door was blocked by the fiery porch, so I ran to the neighbors and dialed 911.

The fire department came and extinguished the blaze and I was requested to explain how it started. I tried to show them the dead time but it had disappeared. For some odd reason the police came and took me in for a lengthy evaluation, and made me feel like a big idiot.

And now, in reading this, you've also killed some time.

What kind of monsters have we become?

PIANO

It was an old, brown, upright piano made in the 1950s. All the keys worked but it needed a slight tuning. Jeff (single male, age 27) would come home every day from work, relax a bit, and go to her. He thought of the piano as his woman, with his fingertips controlling her moods, her responses.

After repeatedly playing the only two songs he had memorized, he would then improvise softly like he was in a trance, inventing bizarre chords and aleatoric (random) melodies. Many of his "sound sculptures" didn't even have a rhythm. At other times he would bang at the keys indiscriminately, playing with raw passion so that it wasn't even actual music in the normal sense of the word. He would lose himself, alone in the music, for hours.

Jeff was proud in his own mind of what he could do but kept it to himself. It gave him an escape from his boring life and the warehouse job, and he felt that playing a musical instrument was important to improve his quality of life and keep his mind from darker things.

One fine summer day, Jeff went to work as usual, leaving open the rear window. Shortly after he drove away, a comical family of beavers crawled through his window in search of fun and adventure.

"Here's a nice piece of wood for chewing apart and taking to the dam." Papa stated upon noticing the piano.

Mama beaver stepped on his tail and said, "Oh no you don't! This is no ordinary piece of wood, Papa. I believe this has a purpose beyond what we see." The children beavers jumped up onto the bench, then the keys, and danced, much to the surprise of their parents. This sounded almost exactly like the noise they heard every evening from their apartment in the nearby creek.

After about a minute Papa yelled, "Enough already! Leave that thing alone!"

Mama retorted, "No, keep dancing; do what I say."

"Don't listen to her, listen to me," Papa shouted.

Mama and Papa glared at each other, and another argument began regarding the best way to deal with their children.

Lars, an unemployed neighbor who knew Jeff was at work, called the sheriff's department.

When the knock came at the door, the quick-thinking parents ran to the basement without bothering the kids. The cops entered via Lars's key and were amused by what they found. Two of the officers brought the kids to the creek without incident while the sheriff closed the window and looked at the piano with pianist envy.

Mama and Papa beaver stayed hidden in the basement until the police left, arguing about money and nagging each other in tones that children don't understand, and then pooped and found their way outside by clawing through the drywall by the back door.

When Jeff returned, his neighbor told him what had occurred and they both had a good laugh together. It amused Jeff to know that he could play as well as, if not somewhat better than, wild beavers.

That evening he smoked something green he bought from local teenagers (they can find anything), went to his piano, and worked on his latest song, "Leck mich im Arsch" by Mozart. It sounded awful, as usual, but he felt really good about himself. He felt he did not have a drug problem because the bud was useful in quieting the voices of his parents who argued in his mind, so he could find his own voice.

The next day, before going to work, he walked to the creek and threw a couple of old harmonicas at the beavers, commanding them to practice so they could have a jam session. The beaver family hid in their home, terrified, until he was long gone and later chewed apart the harmonicas to make this imposed responsibility go away in their own minds.

FLYING HIGH

In his dream, Simon had been flying with outstretched arms through the puffy white clouds and around the high-power lines, zooming about with the confidence of an eagle. It was a great high and he wanted it to continue. Awake now and lying in bed with his girlfriend and his calico cat, he wished he could really fly like that, and continued to ponder it in his daydreaming at work. Was it possible to create something like a surfboard that could interface with the powerful yet delicate magnetic field of the Earth in order to hover above the ground and fly? He became determined to find out.

As autumn went by, Simon bought a used surfboard and a soldering kit and scavenged all kinds of copper and zinc wire, batteries, lasers, and an assortment of who-knows-what electronic and computer stuff. And, of course, rolls of aluminum foil. He stayed up all hours of the night, missed work a lot, and, unfortunately, lost his job. Despite his odd but diligent research he had no positive results.

One day his girlfriend informed him of her plans to leave because of his obsession, his immature fart humor, and because she liked to sleep with the window slightly open and he kept it slightly closed since Simon intensely disliked being cold, so good-bye.

She departed, and his only source of nourishment became junk food, beer, and cheese-puffs. He worked like a man possessed, trying everything imaginable, but the stupid surfboard wouldn't fly. It just sat there like a pile of junk, mocking him.

Two months later, the paunchy, balding sheriff informed him that he was being evicted for non-payment of rent and serious-looking men came and turned off the phone and the water. Then, they disconnected the heat.

At the end of his rope, Simon purchased an illegal, green, leafy substance from certain local teenagers whose identities are being withheld. He reasoned that since a dream had begun this project, a dream was needed to provide the inspiration to finish it.

Late that fateful evening he lit up, inhaled the smoke, and went to his basement in a state of reverie. Guided by otherworldly visions, Simon rewired the board in a complex, new pattern. He adjusted the voltage regulator, applied a larger charge from the battery, and gawked in amazement as the surfboard lifted up off the Ping-Pong table and hovered in mid-air. The cat ran and hid while a deep, electric humming noise, like giant bees on steroids, filled the room.

With joy overflowing, Simon took the surfboard outside and, sitting astride it with a glass fishbowl on his head, applied a slightly higher charge from the car battery strapped to the back of the board. Immediately he felt a rush of wind and watched helplessly as the ground vanished from under his feet. Twenty minutes later, the cold vacuum of space silenced his scream; not exactly what he had in mind in terms of getting high.

The next day, the sheriff returned with a warrant of eviction. He knocked and, receiving no answer, entered through the unlocked door and searched the house, whereupon he found the baggie of leafy material hidden in a smelly old shoe. (Remember, kids, dangerous shoes are illegal here.) A stray bullet frightened the cat into the yard and it ran away without a word. Everyone assumed Simon had skipped out and gone to live with his mom in New York City.

Today, Simon's frozen body rides the surfboard through the solar system, and will likely plunge into the sun in (looking at my watch) four hundred years.

That should warm him up again.

IN THE MOVIES

I used to contemplate what it would be like to go into a movie as it was playing and interact with the characters. Not being one to let a good idea go to waste, I collected together a DVD player, a glass prism, two lasers, three cardboard tubes, and a lot of aluminum foil. I set to work and was soon rewarded with an oddly-shaped contraption that allowed me to teleport into any DVD as it played.

Next, I chose a movie that probably all of us have seen, *The Wizard of Oz*. I popped in the DVD and turned on my machine, which gradually filled the air with light-blue smoke as it warmed up. With a popping noise I was transported in real time into the show, to the beginning, and I was careful not to be seen by a movie camera because that would affect every *Wizard of Oz* movie in existence. I cleverly hid behind scenery and stuff and tried not to be too noticeable.

My first appearance was to Dorothy as she was going home after meeting that guy in the wagon at the start of the film. I yelled at her to stop and warned her that a tornado was coming, but she told me to scram. Thinking it would be worth some money, I asked for an autograph but she ran off faster than I could keep up, and her grungy dog bit my ankle and skedaddled as well.

While attempting to catch up to Dorothy, gale-force winds slowed my progress. All at once the twister grabbed me and set me on the roof of her house as it rotated upwards, and I think I got sick. When we landed, I must have passed out because the next thing I remember was hearing a lot of singing and shouting, and when I searched for Dorothy, she was gone.

The Munchkins were a very rude lot; they accused me of being a witch and chased me from their village down a winding lane. Farther on, some bad-tempered trees threw apples at me as I hurried along, and all the apples had little green worms in them. I got lost repeatedly moving between sets.

When I again caught sight of Dorothy, she had teamed up with three zany companions and was entering the Forbidden Forest. I yelled not to go in, but the girl had probably warned them about me because they all ran away. I followed up to the point where I found scattered piles of straw and a bunch of footprints, and then a creepy winged monkey bit my rear end and flew off.

I didn't feel like climbing a bunch of rocks to the distant castle so I walked to the Emerald City, hoping to meet up with them there. Along the way I remember seeing thousands of flowers and had a strange dream about a lady with a green nose who wanted to hurt me really bad because she felt I was responsible for her empty life and shattered dreams. Finally, I arrived at the gate to the city and the guard wouldn't let me in at first, so I pretended I was a friend of Dorothy's and added that she owed me money.

After a week, they all showed up. I had been partying with the Wizard and my new poppy collection and had convinced the Wiz to send them away. Dorothy's ugly little dog ruined that idea. Toto spotted him behind a curtain and ran over barking, then pulled it aside so the Wizard was visible to everyone. The Scarecrow noticed me behind a different curtain and pointed it out to Dorothy. She called for the movie director, who called the MGM studio security personnel, and they all said hurtful things while kicking my butt and throwing me off the lot.

Once outside the gates of the studio my machine stopped functioning, and with a pop I abruptly found myself back in my living room.

Maybe I'll try *The Matrix* movie next, that might be safer.

THE RABBIT AND THE OWL

It was as fine a summer day as you'd like when an owl named Otus Asio and a rabbit named Sylvi Lagus (nicknamed Quicksilver) met while fishing at the muddy creek that issues from the silvery waterfall that echoes throughout the lush green forest they call home. Suddenly, each wanted to be the one farthest upstream so as to have the choicest selection of the small, delicious fish floating by that had been stunned silly from going over the waterfall. They glared at each other as they moved closer and closer to the falls, attempting to be first in line and ignoring the actual fish they were seeking. Soon they found themselves at the place where the clear, sparkling water came cascading down from high above.

"Ummm, I do believe I was here first," mumbled Quicksilver with an air of superiority.

"Excuse me, but I think you are slightly mistaken," replied Otus in similar fashion.

"Why don't you fly into a car windshield, you mangy jackass!" demanded Quicksilver, his temper rising.

"Indeed! Why don't you go to Mars and eat dirt, you flea-bitten mooncalf!" yelled Otus.

Quicksilver responded, "Oh yeah? Well, here's my impression of your mama," and he twitched and uttered nonsense syllables while grinning like a fool.

Otus retorted, "Really? Here is what your mama looks like," and he limped in a circle and slobbered on himself while gurgling like a baby. Now the argument heated up, and angry words were exchanged as they got madder and madder, occasionally trying to kick each other where it hurts most.

Finally it got to be too much for the colony of bees that lived in a hive attached to a nearby branch who were trying to nap. The Queen sent out her drones to attack, to let those two big idiots know that little more of their bickering would be welcomed. But no sooner had the bees arrived than they found themselves slapped down by the rabbit and the owl, which stopped fussing long enough to eat the bees and notice they were quite tasty if one spit out the stinger.

In a flash of inspiration, Otus flew up in order to capture the entire hive, but Quicksilver had climbed the tree and was contending for the rights to it. More bees came out but Otus and Quicksilver quickly worked together to eat as many as they could. This action so enraged the Queen that she ordered all her bees to flee and not return until 9:30 that evening and most of them made it out. Some built a new hive a mile away and their motto became "Screw that!" which grew into a universal truth throughout the forest although it was the cause of some unrest for quite a while.

Disappointed, the owl and the rabbit returned to the muddy creek and sang old blues tunes and admitted that they weren't that different after all...they both loved blues music. In fact, their favorite musician was Muddy Waters.

Otus related that he had actually found a harmonica once, but it had been chewed apart so it was useless.

The next morning found them back at the creek starting the same power struggle. As they were about to escalate to the kicking stage, a peculiar-looking porcupine named Timmy ambled by and announced he was setting up a local medical practice. Out of kindness, Timmy gave them both a free wellness check and mandatory prostate exam.

That was followed by multiple insurance forms, co-pay information, and medical history questionnaires which completely took their minds off fishing.

CINDERVAMPIRE

Once upon a time there was a widowed lady vampire who married a wealthy, domineering vampire man as her second husband after her first husband died in a freak boating accident. The second husband had two sons who were short and selfish, named Marcos and Silas. By her first husband, the lady had spawned a beautiful daughter, a Goth girl of exquisite goodness and charm, named Samantha.

The stepfather and his sons forced the daughter to be their servant, and she was made to work all the time cooking, cleaning, and doing menial chores like feeding the goats and caring for their pet rabbits. After Samantha's toil was done for the day, she'd return to the small, dusty room given to her and would sing sweetly, like a birdie, out the window for travelers on the nearby road. She would often get up in the morning covered in dust and cinders, hence the nickname Cindervampire. She put up with it all and dared not tell her mother, for the husband had made mother bookkeeper of his Coffin Medicine factory, which kept her very busy.

One fine cloudy day, Albert, Prince of the Vampires, invited everyone to a ball, planning to choose a bride from amongst the ladies. The two mean stepbrothers teased Cindervampire by telling her that ugly ducklings such as her were not invited, and made her weep.

The evening of the party, Marcos and Silas departed for the festivities after locking the poor girl in her room, and Samantha wept again. Her fairy godmother, a werewolf, came to the rescue and performed a jazzy song and dance routine while transforming the young lady from a dowdy damsel to a gorgeous vampiress in a stunning, black-webbed gown with matching boots. The wolf growled and told her she looked good enough to eat.

In order to get her to the ball in style, the werewolf

turned a potato into a fancy black carriage, rabbits into horses, a ferret into a coachman, and frogs into footmen. Then the godmother sent her out to enjoy the party but warned the girl that she was required to return before midnight when the spells would be broken.

At the gathering, the entire crowd was mesmerized by Cindervampire, especially when she got up with the band and sang a few songs. Prince Albert thought her voice sounded familiar and sang a romantic duet with her. Samantha, in turn, became so enchanted by him that she lost track of time and left only at the final toll of the midnight bell, leaving one of her spikey boots on the steps of the palace and flying home as a bat. The Prince ran after her but was too late. Picking up her boot, all he saw was a ferret eating a potato. Again in her room, Samantha graciously thanked the werewolf by giving her a big juicy steak she had taken from the kitchen and carried back in a doggy bag, and the mystical werewolf vanished.

Prince Albert put the boot in a can and vowed to find and marry the girl to whom it belonged. He traveled for weeks, trying the boot on all the women vampires in the kingdom. When he arrived at Cindervampire's castle, the stepbrothers tried in vain to get the Prince to party with them and their poppy collection. Samantha meekly asked if she might try the boot but Marcos and Silas snarled and told her to get lost.

She went crying up to her room and, in desperate hope, sang out the window for the Prince to hear. He ordered that she be brought to him immediately and naturally the boot fit perfectly, so that settled that. The wicked stepbrothers tried to laugh it off but right after the wedding, Prince Albert drove a wooden stake through each of their black, twisted little hearts and cut their heads off with a silver blade.

This angered the rest of the vampires, so Prince Albert and Princess Samantha had to emigrate and find a new castle where they could live happily ever after.

CHOCOLATE BEACH

There is a place I go to in my mind, my happy place, when something hurts my feelings or challenges me beyond my comfort zone and I need to take some deep breaths and escape. It's a beautiful tropical beach where the sand is sugar, the ocean is soda pop, and the palm trees are made of chocolate. Some of the jellyfish are grape while others are apricot, and the fish are fine chocolate on the outside and tasty peanut butter inside and will jump into anyone's hand when called. Everything is free to take and enjoy. I can feel totally at peace with the universe and safely express my innermost thoughts and feelings, and relax and not feel threatened. It's a timeless dream come true (and all non-fattening). I call it Chocolate Beach.

Let's go there now.

OK, we're sitting comfortably on beach chairs under a multi-colored umbrella. The brilliant sun is smiling down and there's a soft, warm breeze on our faces. Gentle waves lap the shore and cotton candy clouds dot the horizon. Farther down the beach, some scantily clad people are playing Frisbee with their dog. They look so happy and won't eat the dog, he's real. We wave to them and they toss us the Frisbee, which I expertly throw back.

While we're absorbed in this tranquil scene, two odd-looking characters walk up from the shoreline and stand near us.

"The time has come," the walrus says, "to speak of many things: of shoes...and ships...and sealing-wax...of cabbages...and kings, I think. Was it kings? Or was it pigs in blankets? I don't remember." He eats oysters with his carpenter friend and they stroll away.

After ten minutes or so, new folks arrive and take the space next to us. Following polite introductions, we continue relaxing as before. However, there's one guy with them, named Lewis, who starts coughing and coughing and can't seem to stop. I wonder what's wrong with him; did something go down the wrong pipe? I don't know but I wish he'd quit it. He finally stops and we go back to enjoying the beach, nibbling on the chocolate palms, very calm and peaceful, and a few minutes later he starts hacking up a lung all over again. To make matters worse, the dog poops where I can see it and nobody cleans it up!

What the heck is going on here? Maybe I should ask Coughing Guy to leave or get help, but I don't go looking for confrontations. I'm trying to be patient but it's getting on my nerves. I turn on the radio but can only get a popular conservative talk show. Lewis starts coughing even louder as he lights up a cigarette, and the stupid dog starts barking at the seagulls and won't shut up. They could at least throw the Frisbee to distract him, is that asking too much?

I'd like to yell at them all to get the hell off my beach, but it's obvious that they're in no rush to leave anytime soon. Then to top it all, some clown in a Jeep starts revving his engine but not going anywhere, just revving his stupid engine in his stupid Jeep.

Sorry, I have to leave; this isn't relaxing anymore. Goodbye, Chocolate Beach, I'll return another time.

You can stay if you want to, my friend, but dammit, I've had all I can take of my happy place for today.

Commentary: This story seemed rather short so to make it longer, here are some letters of the alphabet that you can arrange to make yourself another sentence or two. Abcdeefghijkllmnoopqrstuvvwxyzknirderomenitlavochoc beachnotrealpuworgwon.

A STORY OF DESPAIR

One sunny afternoon, a rude, pint-sized monkey named Mooky was wandering the lush, green forest looking for fun and adventure. He searched every interesting tree hole, cave, and gully but was soon bored out of his gourd. He chased his tail, which held his interest for about ten minutes, and then ambled around aimlessly. At noon he had a drink of water from a peaceful stream and, feeling sleepy, Mooky sat himself down in a cool glen under a shady dogwood tree.

Dozing off, he dreamed that his ex-girlfriend was rubbing his belly and being playful. He smiled and told her how much he liked her. She kept rubbing his belly and he was enjoying it very much until he woke up and discovered the shocking truth. Four mischievous young bunnies had gathered and were rubbing his furry belly with their tiny paws and giggling softly. He shrieked and jumped up in surprise, and cursed at them. They immediately scattered and Mooky pursued them back to their hole in the ground that appeared to be guarded by a large cow named Ernie.

"Stop," cried Ernie in a husky voice as Mooky tried to enter. "No monkeys are allowed down there!"

"Get the hell out of my way!" yelled Mooky. "I have to get even with those damn rabbits; they made a fool of me. I am soooooo maaaaad!! Now move it, let me in!"

"Well ain't that a shame, poor little monkey. Now scram, get out of here!" replied Ernie. The monkey was now extremely angry at this stupid bovine which he felt was trying to micromanage his life. He was so mad he could not think straight.

"What are you, high? You're not the boss of me!" shouted Mooky. With that, the monkey ran around the cow to sneak in the other way, but every time he did the cow was there baring his fangs, looking very fierce, and barking ferociously. At least, I think it was a cow.

After five minutes of this, the monkey ran away discouraged and climbed a nearby tree to be alone. He experienced intense despair and wondered if he'd ever be able to relax again. He felt he was having a relapse of Chronic Pervasive Disorder and knew with regret he'd have to make an appointment to see his doctor. Mooky took several big swallows from his secret hip flask, and then stared at his hands with his mind a blank and his feelings numb for a long time, wondering why his life was not a bed of roses.

Snapping out of his funk, he hurled three oranges at Ernie and cussed him out. He called the rabbits bad names and made indecent comments about their mothers. Then he yelled to anyone who would listen as to what he imagined was really going on inside their nest in the ground - all kinds of vile perversions - and worked himself into a frenzy. The various animals that happened by ran off in disgust. Even Ernie (the cow, I think) could stand it no longer so he left and was not seen for weeks.

By this time all the rabbits were hopping mad so Quicksilver, the president-elect of the rabbits, popped out of the hole and expertly hurled a rock at Mooky, knocking him off his perch and into the brush below. As the monkey hit the ground, he banged his head against a hard root and lay there, stunned. For a few moments he felt remorse over his choice of words. In a flash, all the rabbits rushed out of their burrow and stoned him to death, then cooked and ate him (except for his head, which they put in a jar for their museum).

I know this is a violent ending so if you are offended, pretend Mooky survived and ran away to join the circus. Maybe you'll get your wish.

Commentary: See, getting stoned is not always good.

LIFE ON MARS

You wouldn't have expected it, but Mars is being populated by mice. The Lizard People who control NASA are shooting them up there, first on those space-probes, and now on secret missiles. I could get in big trouble for telling you this because millions of dollars have already been wasted, I mean spent. I know that the government is raising them covertly in the mountains near Denver, Colorado.

These rodents have been conditioned to eat dirt and survive on less oxygen than usual in order to endure the harsh conditions of the fourth planet from the sun. The mice on Mars are currently building a concrete runway in the middle of a great plain so that one day we can safely land there, conquer any Martians that might exist, and rule with an iron fist until they start a bloody revolution, turn the tables, and capture all our equipment and enslave our people.

But what happens if the mice on Mars revolt first and want the whole planet for themselves? Would we have to send up an army of cats? After that, naturally we'd send up an army of dogs to take the planet away from the cats. We'd have to rename Mars and call it Fido, the Dog Planet. Perhaps we'd send that dog-trainer guy who was on TV to be their pack leader. Then it would be his planet. Would he share it with us? Possibly not....

If that's the case, I suggest parachuting in a squad of heavily armed fashion models wearing fur parkas with bags of doggie treats, and a camera crew. I think they could win Mars back without too much trouble. Of course, everyone would have to live in Colorado first to get used to the thin atmosphere and learn to eat dirt. But, what if the models didn't want the rest of us up there and wanted the runway all for themselves? We'd be in a real pickle! We could try to bomb them from across the vast distance of space, but if we killed them all we'd have to send up more mice and start the whole process over.

Wait, instead of mice, send up donkeys wearing neat and pressed uniforms, maybe gray and yellow, with epaulettes where their shoulders should be, and striped pants. They would be single-minded and do their work efficiently. Yes, I like that idea. But then, what if they, too, had a change of heart and didn't want us to use their new runway? What if they wanted the whole damn planet for themselves? Mars might become the Donkey Planet with a leader named Kong. We'd be in a real pickle again!

I considered different combinations of animals that might be sent together to keep an eye on each other: aardvarks and warthogs, tawny owls and fluffy rabbits, panda bears and llamas (and which uniforms they could wear), but the more I reflected, the less sense it made until my thoughts were swirling like a strawberry smoothie in a blender. It was almost as if an alien intelligence was interfering with my creativity. I have to be careful about that because I don't want people to see past my normal demeanor and think I'm some sort of idiot. (Gee, I hope I didn't say that out loud.) So to resume:

I suppose we could send up apes to round up the donkeys and continue the work. We could first teach them to play table tennis so during their free time they wouldn't think of blowing up the runway. They'd have to train near Denver, and possibly learn to grow different kinds of fungus so they wouldn't have to eat dirt all the time. They'd appreciate that, but...what if the apes rebelled and took over anyway; what would we call Mars then? Planet of the Apes? No, that's already been used. How about Planet of the Simians?

Forget it. Just keep the name Mars. This is all making me depressed and I don't give a damn anymore.

FOOD FOR THOUGHT

It was a hot and humid day in August when Dickey, a field mouse, finished chewing out a home for his family in the bottom of a telephone pole. It had been difficult because those poles are treated with powerful chemicals to make them resist the elements, so at the end of his efforts Dickey had a migraine headache and blurry vision. After moving in, his family also experienced dizziness and nausea now and then. It wasn't long before all the children came down with a bad case of Chronic Pervasive Disorder and had to be taken to the local doctor, a porcupine. He smelled bad and cussed a lot, but his prices were reasonable because he wasn't part of any managed health care system.

The mice lived a few miles outside of town so there were lots of open areas to go searching for food. They enjoyed eating insects, vegetables, and discarded Taco Bell; other times they were thinking Arby's. They would have tried McDonald's but the owls and raccoons always beat them to it. Of course, there were lots of cats, birds, and snakes to beware of. Life is not always as simple as it seems. Trust me on that.

Late one afternoon, as Dickey Mouse was searching for dinner, he noticed a passing shadow that indicated immediate danger. An owl named Otus was circling overhead and had spotted him. The little guy ran as fast as he could for shelter but as he was scurrying along, he got one of his headaches. This caused him to become disoriented and he stumbled and fell, enabling the owl to capture him. Dickey squeaked for all he was worth as the bird carried him to its nest.

Before it ate him, Dickey warned the feathered fiend of all the strange chemicals in his body and explained how it might make the bird sick. He was hoping for mercy, which is a rare trait in the animal kingdom. Otus totally ignored his plea and devoured the unhappy mouse, tail and all, while listening to his favorite Johann Strauss Jr. melody, the overture to "Deflate-a-mouse."

The next morning the bird awoke feeling nauseous. Then he became dizzy and developed a bad migraine headache. One might have noticed sparks shooting out of his butt, almost like in a cartoon, as one watched him hopping repeatedly from one foot to the other.

The owl froze, blinked hard several times, and declared, "Wait a minute! My name is Dickey. I'm not a bird, I'm a mouse, and I miss my family!" Upon this realization he soared into the air and flew in wide circles until he found what he was searching for.

He dove toward the telephone pole where his family was waking up, landed clumsily, and tried to enter the too-small hole to their home while calling them by name. He even brought along three McDonald's French fries he'd found the day before and had been saving. The mama mouse and young ones freaked out and ran in circles inside their cubbyhole, crying in desperation. The bird continued to proclaim that he was Dickey Mouse, finally coming home, but this made the mice even more confused. The fries were out of reach for the rodents and the tantalizing aroma made them extremely hungry.

The owl could not get in because of his size and the mice dared not come out. It was a stalemate so Dickey, to prove who he was, started telling them about his rodent genealogy and going back ten generations. Next, he recounted all his trips to the doctor and every ache and pain he had had since he was a pup. Then he started in about his comic book collection.

Hours later, out of the maddening frustration of listening to Dickey drone on and on without a break, the hungry mice ran out, and, being an owl, Dickey ate them...and the fries. Later on he felt guilty for what he had done so he threw them up.

As they say, you are what you eat.

MY DINOSAUR

I had been digging in my backyard, looking for loose change, when I found what appeared to be a very old piece of shell and I wondered if it might actually be from an ancient dinosaur egg. I needed to know so I brought it inside to my basement laboratory and by means of a secret process involving aluminum foil, lasers, and a tiny pair of zircon-encrusted tweezers I extracted what DNA I could and implanted it in the cat. Nine months later my dinosaur was born.

He looked like a miniature, furry version of Godzilla and had razor-sharp teeth so kitty refused to nurse him. I had to hand-feed him, and soon my hands were covered in bandages.

I named him Spikey.

He grew and grew and when he was about the size of a pygmy pony I went to get a license for him. The clerk at City Hall was quite skeptical and told me I didn't need a license for a dinosaur. Let him laugh, it saved me some money.

Well, one day the cat disappeared, then the neighbor's dog mysteriously vanished, and I noticed food missing from the refrigerator. Due to his unresolved Edible Complex, Spikey was yearning for his mom while eating everything in sight and getting bigger and bigger. The messes he made in the backyard – don't even go there!

I planned on starting Dinosaur Island, a kind of zoo where people could come to tease and throw food at him but quickly found out I didn't have the capital for the start-up expenses. I thought about letting Spikey go free but I'm sure somebody else would have captured him and created a different Dinosaur Island, ripping off my idea.

That's when I came up with Plan B. I could throw a saddle on him and let folks ride him around for five bucks while chained to a post at carnivals and renaissance fairs.

By this time he was the size of a Buick so I bought a cheap saddle, strapped it on him, and we were ready for business. By the way, the insurance was going to be prohibitively expensive so I listed him as a giant mouse, and they told me I didn't need insurance for a mouse. Let them laugh. Regrettably, he attacked each person who tried to ride him so there was only one thing left to do. I called the Dinosaur Whisperer.

Weeks later, what an improvement! Spikey was transformed into a friendly, gentle dinosaur beloved by everyone who met him. I took him on the Tonight Show and on one of those confrontational daytime talk shows. We became famous, especially after he had a relapse and attacked the host with a folding metal chair. Spikey did not appreciate appearing alongside guests who cross-dress as small furry animals and authors who cheat on their taxes. There was also a taxidermist with a guilty secret who kept staring at us, making Spikey extremely uncomfortable.

Spike also appeared on T-shirts, lunchboxes, and did a commercial for a diet cola drink I can't legally name anymore. I was finally showing a profit. Then, sad to say, he became tired and sickly. A trip to the local veterinarian revealed that my prickly friend had come down with...Reptile Dysfunction.

Spikey is getting old much faster than normal due to the atmosphere – too much darn oxygen. So let's all get together, burn leaves and garbage, and pollute the air and oceans as much as possible, and have many more babies. Please, do it for Spikey.

Now that I think of it, I may also need money for his monument so any donation you wish to send me will be greatly appreciated.

GETTING OLDER

Weird Charles stood extremely close to the bathroom mirror, staring at his tired reflection in the morning light. There was no doubt – the mole was getting bigger. It was brown, the size of a pencil eraser, on his neck an inch below his jawbone on the left side. His mind told him things he did not want to hear. He was getting older and wiser, for sure, but he did not want to get older. He wanted to stay young and healthy, not turn into a grizzled old grandpa with arthritis, wrinkles, moles, and hair growing out of strange places. As a side note, he enjoyed seeing how many different weird faces he could make at himself in the mirror (try it sometime…seriously).

Charles was also one of those individuals who compulsively counted objects and attempted to make the count come out to an even number. Even was good, odd was bad, and he presumed everyone understood that. In fact, he was so sure that others would be mocking him for only having one mole that he decided to see a doctor.

Dr. Carol was at her desk when Charles burst into her private office with the receptionist at his heels, telling him he needed an appointment. He sat in a chair and said, "You're a real doctor, right?" Dr. Carol tried not to appear alarmed and assessed him silently. The receptionist continued to scold him and when Charles refused to budge, she left to phone the police.

He smiled at the doctor, using his telepathy on her and tapping his chin nervously with his fingers. He turned his head to give her a view of the mole but wasn't sure how to put things into words other than, "I have an odd problem." A very perceptive Dr. Carol was staring at Charles to see what he would do next when she noticed the mole.

"I can help you," she stated plainly. "You must have that mole removed from your neck or have another one like it on the other side." Charles stopped breathing. She understood! (By a strange coincidence you will only find here, when she was younger she also had this obsession but had mostly grown out of it. Come to think of it, I'm pretty sure most people actually do believe even is better than odd, so maybe not such a coincidence after all?)

"I was hoping you would understand," he said. Dr. Carol stood up and walked around to examine his mole. Yep, it could easily be removed, but would be quite expensive because her practice was part of a huge health maintenance organization run by hundreds of over-paid administrators who did nothing but invent elaborate billing codes to impress their insurance company friends.

"May I see your ID and insurance card?" she asked politely in order to schedule an MRI and a series of blood tests and other unnecessary diagnostics.

"Oh, I don't need insurance," he chuckled, thinking of his huge, empty water bottle at home filled with coins. Charles confided to her that he had been monitoring Mr. Mole closely in the mirror for months, whereupon she counseled him that if one stands too close to the mirror, one does not get the full picture of who one is. It went right over his head.

Dr. Carol sat down and Charles shared with her some of his unique mirror faces and bombarded her with more telepathic messages until the police arrived. The cops took him and his mole to the station and locked them in a pink padded cell.

A day later he went before a judge who had a similar mole. Charles imagined that the judge was mocking him, and grew angry. He was convicted of trespassing and sentenced to psychiatric counseling and time served.

On his way out of the courtroom, Weird Charles turned and shouted, "Mole! Mole! Mole!" at the old judge until he was out of earshot.

Yes, he was getting older, but not much wiser.

REVENGE

In long procession marched the villagers up the dark, remote mountainside trail. Some carried torches, others had pitchforks, and one had a 3/8" socket torque wrench. Revenge was in the heart of each man as they marched to the castle wherein lived an old woman and her adult son, and the woman was accused of practicing witchcraft. Five of the teenage girls in the village had been caught laughing and dancing the tarantella like rabid monkeys, and they swore the old woman had turned into a fox and given them a large red apple that had been bewitched to make them lose their self-control. Living so far from other villages, the superstitious locals had changed very little over the course of centuries, except for that wrench.

Upon arriving, the mob observed the high dark walls and mighty gate that stood before them. The massive door was locked and bolted and the castle was impregnable from any other direction – further evidence of their guilt, the villagers concluded. The dark figures worked at prying the hinges from the wooden door but their efforts went slowly because they had brought inadequate tools, much to their dismay.

The occupants, who had recently arrived from another country, heard the commotion and by listening closely, discerned the reason for this nocturnal raid.

"So, I'm a witch, am I?" cackled the old woman. They climbed to the parapet above and the son, in his bathrobe, called out, "Hey, you kids get the hell off my lawn!" He was ignored and the work continued.

The mother turned to her son and asked sarcastically, "Friends of yours?"

"I don't have any friends, thanks to you, mother." he replied. "Now why did you have to dress up in a fox costume and give an apple to those girls in town? Why do you always go out looking for trouble?"

"I did it because I'm foxy!" she said, feeling defensive. "And it made me feel special. So tell me why that fellow helping attack us is waving your socket wrench at me."

"Who the heck knows," he mumbled. She would never understand his secret addiction to the white horse, selling his tools to buy more, and he was dealing with all the guilt he felt by withdrawing and blaming others for his problem. Meanwhile, the massive door was refusing to budge. The son ran to his office to look for weapons.

When he returned with a bow and arrows he took aim at the group below, but he really didn't want to hurt anyone so he froze. Then, in a desperate flash of brilliance, he called out, "Ho there! If I throw you down the old witch, will you promise to leave and never return?" The villagers stopped and stared upward. After several minutes of hushed murmurs, one of them responded, "Betcha ya do and we'll go away, I tells ya dat."

"OK," the son yelled back, "Give her a minute to say her prayers, and then over she goes. But as she falls, I'm going to put a curse on her." With that, he ran and grabbed the mannequin from the attic, threw an old dress and wig on it, and tossed it over the wall.

As it hurtled earthward he screamed, "Vescere bracis meis, hominis!" and the dummy hit the ground. The men had never seen a mannequin before and assumed it was the body of the witch. Instantly they fled in horror.

Back at the village the sun was rising as the mob returned home to learn the truth. The teens had admitted overnight that they lied concerning the old woman in order to make excuse for their own sensual gratification. For punishment, they were led to the middle of the town square with burlap sacks over their heads, and put in the stocks in nothing but their frilly underwear for a day.

The foxy old woman and her son moved away two months later to a rehab facility in California and sold the castle to a couple of real-life vampires who had recently arrived from a distant land.

ALL FOR NOTHING

Eventually there was an elderly owl named Otus who loved to fly around and feed on the hapless creatures scurrying along on the ground trying not to be seen. He especially loved to eat mice. Otus would sleep most of the day and get up before sundown to prepare his route maps so that on every expedition he covered a different area.

His family doctor, a porcupine named Timmy, had advised him to get extra rest, drink plenty of fluids, and "Take it easy, you dirty old bird." Otus often wondered how much the doc understood about owls so he didn't take all the pills prescribed for him. The owl also avoided the doctor whenever possible because he didn't appreciate the cat scans (using real cats) or the frequent prostate exams Timmy insisted upon.

All the mice knew to hide when they heard Otus coming but since owls are essentially soundless when they fly, it was most difficult. Many mice had lost family members to the owl and that irked them. It was a shame, they reasoned, that they couldn't "take him out" somehow, and different plans were brainstormed.

They gnawed twigs and branches and made a cage to trap him, but Otus was too smart to enter it, even for the wooden decoy mice. They mailed him travel brochures to faraway places, but he refused to take the hint.

Then one day the mice chanced upon a picture of a bow and arrow in a magazine that some human had discarded. All the mice skilled in engineering studied the image and set about gnawing the components needed for the device. They love to gnaw and even have special music for it from a rodent rock band named "Sha-gnaw-gnaw."

It took several months, but eventually they crafted their own makeshift bow and arrow out of branch and twine. What they needed now was opportunity. The mice spent two weeks tracking Otus and were able to discover where he roosted. Afterwards, the mice statisticians collected data and did a study to determine the optimal time to take their shot. The bow was positioned and the string drawn back to create the potential energy needed to fire the weapon. That was the hardest part. The engineers were clever little critters, and how they did it we shall never know. They were all ready now to gnaw at the catch-string to release the deadly arrow.

Evening was approaching as Otus roused himself from a frequent nightmare about eating his own children. He yawned and stretched his tawny wings, but before he could collect his thoughts an arrow came whizzing by and lodged in the bark less than an inch from his head.

"Hello," he exclaimed in surprise. "Hello, what's this?" The bird blinked hard several times then looked around and saw the mice scurrying off with the bow.

"Oh crap!" Otus shouted. The owl was waxing wroth as he flew out and swooped down to take it away from the mice. At the exact moment he clutched the bow in his talons, he died of a massive heart attack from not taking his cholesterol medicine.

The mice stopped and stared at him for two minutes before one of them whispered, "Heart attack? All that work for nothing?" Then they threw a celebration party and ate him without thinking of the consequences.

If you don't like that ending, imagine they gave him a solemn burial and returned home, but the rest of us will know the truth and live with it.

Commentary: The best laid plans of mice and men often go awry.

TAKING OVER THE WORLD

I think that every person has, at some point in time, thought how cool it would be to become emperor of the world; to be able to tell everyone else what to do. It appealed as a harmless fantasy but the question was how.

First, I assumed that if I simply asked nicely, that would do the trick, but wrong. I realized I might be a borderline big idiot for being so naïve. Other people are too inherently selfish to freely accommodate my every whim.

Second, I reasoned that if I had enough hydrogen bombs, I could force the world to follow my commands, but if a few smart-alecks called my bluff I'd have to explode them all over strategic oil fields. Who'd want to obey me after that? Plus, that's a bit unrealistic, to say the least. No, I needed something that was subtler, more devious, and yet practical. Then I recognized what the key was. Music! The public loves music and since I'm a bit of a musician, that was my best bet.

I cleared the fern plants from my synthesizer, hooked up the four-track recorder, and let my hands play aimlessly across the keys as if in a trance with my eyes closed. On another track I recorded the whispered words "Obey me" at random intervals. I did this for several hours, adding layers of different tracks. Of course, I used my aluminum foil hat to help me focus.

Later, after mixing all the channels into one, I had something I wouldn't quite call real music, but it was mesmerizing in a bizarre kind of way and ready for testing. I had my roommate give a listen, and made copies for my other three friends. After a while the effect took hold, and what happened next was truly amazing.

My friends began asking if there was anything they could do for me, so I had them make copies to give to *their* friends and pass it along like a chain letter. Apparently I had hit upon the exact combination of sounds, probably a one in ten gazillion chance, which actually enabled me to control others.

About a week later, all sorts of men and women began showing up at my house all hours of the day and night, asking for instructions, and it became really annoying. I tried to think of things for them to do, like pull up weeds and wash my van for me. Some got weird and started chanting my name. A few thought I lived in the house next door to mine and camped on the lawn, but my neighbor-lady put an end to that with her garden hose.

A few days later, so many people had gathered that they were blocking the street with their cars and trucks. I was about to command them to do what I call the "underwear dance" when the police arrived. I begged the officers to listen to my tape but that was an exercise in futility. Everyone claimed I had forced him or her to come there, and I was given a citation and fined for causing a public disturbance.

The sheriff, wanting to get back to his dinner, fired a few stray shots from his service revolver into the air. The neighbor-lady screamed and the crowd rapidly dispersed. I spread the word to dispose of the tapes and the effects eventually wore off.

I'm starting to wonder, do I want to be in control of the whole world? It seems like a lot of work. I have enough problems of my own without having to make decisions for a bunch of strangers.

You may be thinking of all my missed opportunities, like getting a girlfriend, having people buy me beer and cigarettes and giving me money, but I was too busy trying to sort out my own powers, responsibilities, and personal demons to think of that.

Maybe next time.

SOME PARTY!

In a faraway part of the Mystee forest there lived a martini-drinking cow named Ernie, a clever rabbit called Quicksilver, and a mangy old tiger named Scraps. One finite summer day, around two in the afternoon, the cow was feeling a bit hungry. Since cows secretly love to eat rabbits, Ernie telephoned every rabbit in the phone directory to see who would answer. Finally, someone did.

"Oh crap," thought Quicksilver, hearing Ernie's voice.

"Hey, come to my…li'l party," said the cow, slurring his words. "I have a fun new game we can play. This is Ernie, your friend." Ernie belched into the phone.

Quicksilver reflected before responding. After all, his wife and kids had recently been to one of the cow's parties and hadn't been seen since, nor her gold pendant.

"Um, OK Mr. Cow, be over soon," he replied, and hung up. The rabbit thought a bit and called his cousin, Scraps the tiger, at the brewery and told him of an idea he had. The tiger might go to the party disguised as Quicksilver in order to see what would take place and maybe find out what happened to his family and many missing friends. It seemed like a good idea so Scraps finished labeling another pallet of Old Warthog beer, went and rented a rabbit suit and gloves, and set out for the cow pasture.

On his way he passed an old she-goat that asked in a sing-song voice, "Where are you going this finite day with yourself all dressed up like that?"

"I'm going to some party with Ernie the cow. Come on along," said the tiger cheerfully. The goat agreed and hobbled happily along behind Scraps. After a half hour of travel and light conversation, they arrived at the pasture where the mischievous cow was sunning himself and getting buzzed on dirty martinis.

"Hello, Mr. Cow," said the tiger in a high, thin voice.

"That's a very nice gold pendant you have around your neck, may I ask where you got it?"

"Hello there, runny babbit...bunny fabbit...furry runny mabbit...bammit, umm...hi," mumbled the cow, unaware of much besides the spinning pasture and his own big feet.

"Is it party time?" asked Scraps as tension filled the air. The goat glanced around sheepishly then ran like a scaredy-cat to the house on the hill.

"Cow hungry!" bellowed Ernie, regaining some of his composure and staring off into the distance. "Come here and put this apple in your mouth," he ordered, baring his teeth. Scraps took a running start and jumped onto the cow's back, tipping him over and spilling his drink.

"Looky here," roared Scraps, "I am the King of the Rabbits and I'm here to find out what's going on."

"What?" Ernie said.

"I want to know what's been going on here."

"What?" Ernie said again.

"What have you been doing with these rabbits?"

"What?" Ernie repeated, suppressing a smile.

"You heard me!" Scraps yelled.

"Who is John Galt?" asked Ernie.

"I don't know…. Look, I'm a rabbit. See the ears and the tail? Tell me about your parties. I hear you really like bunnies, right?"

"What?" Ernie said, starting to giggle.

"You're beginning to piss me off, you drunken cow! I suspect they're all dead if you're the kind of mad cow that likes to eat rabbits."

"What?"

Ten minutes later, the old goat returned with two unsuspecting chickens carrying a pot of water only to witness the tiger chasing the cow across the infinite horizon and heard the distant cry of "Cow hungry."

"Oh crap," said the goat sarcastically, "some party!"

REALITY TV

There are a lot of reality shows on television these days. Many of them are scripted fakes designed for ratings and advertising dollars which feature obnoxious people and expose them to our derision. But a few, like those dealing with home renovation, are interesting and better than most of the gory violence and brainwashing that has taken over what used to be called news and entertainment (my opinion). I'd much rather see audiences exposed to people working design and construction instead of breaking the law, but ultimately freedom means free to make bad choices, and Rome must have its Colosseum.

But today, whether it's survival, dating, cooking, or whatever, our voyeuristic, adrenaline-addicted culture has embraced these reality shows. Of course, dating and cooking both involve differing degrees of survival. So, what would it be like to watch a big network show that combines this with their crime shows that are currently popular? It might go like the following:

Our camera crew is at a busy downtown intersection with film equipment hidden inside a minivan with darkened windows. It's a warm summer afternoon and the lunch-hour traffic is bustling. Our actor, Paul, wearing a hoodie, is coming from behind our parked vehicle to hijack a car while we film it. OK, it's a middle-aged woman in a red SUV who has stopped at the traffic light next to us. Paul points the gun at her and yells to get out. She's startled for a moment, and then screams, jumps out of the SUV, and runs off. Did you see the look on her face? That was priceless!

Now our producer is running after her so she can sign the release form in order for us to use this segment on our show. Oh look, she just slapped him in the face and is walking back. Paul tries to ask her for a date but she gives him a swift kick to his shinbone, screeches obscenities, and squeals the tires as she speeds away. Was that a baby in her backseat? It simply goes to show that some people shouldn't be in the entertainment industry.

We wait cheerfully for our next unsuspecting reality star. This time it's a man who drives up in a Jeep, dressed as a clown, probably on his way to a children's party. I'll bet clowns are good at taking jokes. Paul limps over to his door, flashes the gun, and commands him to get out. They appear to be arguing and it's taking longer than usual. Suddenly the clown pulls out a handgun and shoots Paul in the shoulder, then speeds away.

There will be a short break while our producer pulls the bullet out with a pair of needle-nose pliers and bandages him up. We were not able to get the subject to sign a release, so this segment won't be useable either. You'd think clowns would have more respect for people, right? I guess we won't get to see which pie in the face tastes better.

We decide to do one additional taping before taking Paul to the hospital to stop the bleeding. This time a big, fancy Cadillac pulls up, driven by an old guy wearing a fedora. Paul staggers around our van and feebly waves the gun, motioning for the guy to get out. The man rolls down his window and says a few words, following which Paul beckons to us and our producer steps over to greet the gentleman. The old guy slowly explains that he is a well-connected member of a powerful crime organization with ties to City Hall. Our producer quickly clarifies that this is a humorous reality television show, and we were going to offer to send him into the wilderness for survival training.

The man calmly points out that we are now targeted for a "hit" so we pack up for the day, go home to collect a few essentials, and all go into hiding in the wilderness.

Commentary: Maybe that's a little too real. It seems my story is no better than the shows I condemn.

BEACH HOLIDAY

Little Mikey and his mom and dad were motoring their way to the ocean and Mikey could hardly sit still, even though he was strapped extra tightly into the car seat in back.

"Are we there yet?" was all he could think of to say. Although he was driving his parents crazy, they were being tolerant. It was going to be the perfect beach holiday. Mikey was being rewarded for going a whole week without fighting with his big sister or throwing a tantrum, and she had to stay home. The psychologist told his parents that they needed to reward his good behavior if they wanted to unspoil him and enjoy more happy-days.

They arrived and found a parking space in the front row. Dad opened the trunk, and he and Mom took out their beach stuff, a few books, and the wine-coolers. Their 6 year-old son got his swim gear and sand toys and carried them proudly as they found an ideal spot on the sand near the waterline. Mom and Dad set up the umbrella and chairs, applied suntan lotion, and settled in for a warm, sunny day of fun and relaxation.

The boy immediately went to the water's edge to look for anything crawling or swimming around, and then stared at the gulls circling overhead. Mikey started building a sandcastle, digging and molding the sand with his plastic tools. Completed, it was tall and intricate and his parents were impressed. He dug a space around it which he filled with several pails of water to create a moat. Then, he imagined it was being attacked by mutated red crabs that he repelled with fistfuls of sand bombs. Tiring of that, the lad waded into the sea up to his chest and splashed as Mom looked on approvingly.

A short while later, they heard the beach siren that indicated someone had spotted a shark, and everybody was scrambling to get out of the water. The lifeguards were running back and forth, shouting and frantically blowing their whistles, so Mom walked to the waterline and ordered Mikey to return. He ignored her. Wanting the fun to continue, he waded farther out until he was on his tippy toes and swam off laughing. Seeing the approaching fin, Mom screamed, "Shark" and Dad came running into the water with the only weapons he had.

Mikey saw the huge fin and froze in amazement. It passed by not more than ten feet away. Dad was moving as fast as he could and Mom was panic-stricken. The big fish came around once more and as it passed between him and the boy, Dad jumped the shark to steer it away from his idiot son, yelling and beating its fin with a wine-cooler bottle. That seemed to have no effect, so he leaned forward and jammed his pocket dictionary up the creature's nose. The huge man-eater was annoyed enough to turn and head away from shore with Dad riding it like a horse. Mom continued to scream and Mikey returned to her in tears. A lifeguard in a motorboat followed Dad and was able to rescue him when he slipped off the shark. The monster continued out to deeper water with a sore fin and the urge to sneeze. While returning to shore, Dad thought of a few choice words to say to their family psychologist.

When Mikey was reunited with his family, they figured out a fitting punishment. Mom and Dad took turns kicking in his sandcastle and recorded it on their cell phones, then posted it to a social media website where it went viral because of their laughter and the forlorn look on Mikey's surprised face.

Feelings started boiling up within him. Mom and Dad didn't care about his fun or his feelings, and he hadn't done anything wrong. In fact, nothing bad had happened to anyone but him. Just before his meltdown he realized that, somehow, this was all his sister's fault.

FUZZY TURTLES

Somewhere in the Mystee forest there lived a herd of big, fuzzy turtles; the fuzz being the result of no one ever sweeping the forest floor. Their leader was named King Egbert, and he had become king by being voted the biggest and fuzziest turtle of them all. His Majesty was writing his autobiography because he recognized that when he was old and no longer king, he would need the book revenue to help care for his wonderful wife and make a few home repairs. There was no salary for life after his term was over. (He also needed a good editor.)

Egbert was famous for his proverbs; one was "If you stand too close to your reflection, you cannot see the full picture of who you are." My favorite was "Always keep your mouth closed when cleaning the toilet." (I used to have the full list, I'll look for it.) He could be very profound, as well as humorous.

One chilly afternoon in early October, King Egbert and his friends were out looking for food in the soft sunlight that filtered through the leaves. Scattered about the forest were lots of apples, lettuce, celery and walnuts for them to consume freely. They occasionally discussed whether or not they were actually tortoises, but were quite certain they were turtles since every time one of them asked another if he or she was a turtle, the other would reply, "You bet your sweet ass I am!"

All of a sudden, a long line of rabbits came racing through their territory as fast as they could run, and many a turtle was flipped unceremoniously onto his or her back in the rush. Just as quickly as they had appeared, the rabbits were gone. Everyone was stunned at this unwarranted incursion, and hours were spent helping upside-down turtles regain their footing. This occurred again a few days later. A conference was called, and King Egbert brought the group to order by banging his gavel on his secretary's back.

"Friends, turtles, countrymen," he announced loudly, and began to shake a spear.

"We need a hoppy ending to this situation. Look, I'm not going to split hares, but we need to stick our necks out and take action. I suggest we string piano wire across that trail and stop those speeding fur-balls once and for all!" An argument ensued regarding tactics. At first they were at loggerheads, but after a snappy discussion the turtles agreed to purchase a piano and a huge party was held at the Fuzzy Logic Tavern in anticipation of their victory.

A few days later, after they had all sobered up, they bought a cheap piano online. When it arrived they hired beavers to chew it apart, took out the wires, and stretched the longest ones across the rabbit path. And sure enough, here came the rabbits. Traveling rapidly, the ones in front were tripped up and they all piled on top of one another, causing great confusion and making them all late.

The angry rabbits shouted, "F__ you, you f__ing turtles!"

The angry turtles that had hidden themselves in the brush along the trail rushed out to attack while shouting, "F__ you, you f__ing rabbits!" but by the time they reached the pile-up the rabbits had recovered and were sprinting away.

The rabbits chose to take a different route in the future and this was seen as a major victory by the turtles and they celebrated like before. A week later, His Majesty's Secretary advertised for a literary agent to help spread King Egbert's fame far beyond that faraway fuzzy forest. Unfortunately, all they got was a big fat idiot named Norbert who claimed to be an agent, who demanded money up front and then disappeared. King Egbert needs your help now to spread the word of his book.

(No animals were hurt in the writing of this story. And since all turtles are polite, the capital F stands for Forget and the small f stands for forage.)

HAND PUPPETS

It has always been my belief that we do not use enough hand puppets in our daily lives, whether to add flair to a conversation, enhance a sales pitch, or for a little comic relief. I think puppets make the world a better place because they are amusing and help us take ourselves less seriously. Think of how they could cheer up victims of natural disasters like hurricanes and tornados.

With this in mind, I took an old white sock and, with a magic marker, drew on eyes and a funny nose and named it Mr. Sock. I took it everywhere and used it to talk through at opportune times, like a ventriloquist's dummy. It allowed me to be funny and yet say important things I am normally reluctant to say, like, "get a job", "chew with your mouth closed" and "stop staring at me." I also used it at job interviews and when trying to get a date. However, Mr. Sock was not at all politically correct and a few times got me in trouble, like when we had to stand in the waiting line at the unemployment office. Those people don't cheer up easily.

Eventually, the puppet got fed up with me putting words in its mouth and one day it began putting words in my mouth, expressing itself through me. I told Mr. Sock that he was being unreasonable but the thing had a mind of its own by then. I wondered if I was headed for the loony bin but Mr. Sock calmly assured me I wasn't. He claimed that scientifically, I was merely an extension of *his* personality and I needed to keep him on my hand permanently. According to the sock, I still had a lot to learn about the nature of consciousness.

He sounded like an authority, so I thought, "OK, let's see what happens." The first thing he made me do was give him most of the money in my savings account. Second, I had to create an online identity and website for him. Then he began to micromanage my life, telling me what I could and couldn't do, which I didn't like.

Mr. Sock deprived me of food and sleep and often repeated the same thoughts over and over to make me memorize his views. He cursed and was mean to me when I resisted and even punched me on my other arm a few times. (I'm glad I didn't draw any teeth in his mouth!)

He proclaimed that my family and friends were my enemies since they didn't share "our" goal of making the world a better place through sock puppets. I had to discontinue all contact with them and only associate with people who spoke through puppets. This supposedly makes me happy.

Our new movement, called Puppetology, is growing quickly, recruiting followers at airports, colleges, and through a thick book that makes outrageous claims. Luckily, some people will believe anything that's printed in a book. Trust me, it is not a church and we don't prey on the insecure looking for meaning in life...not much, anyway.

Several average Hollywood stars joined and gave us lots of money without being blackmailed, so now we're better able to spread the word and buy expensive office furniture and hire security staff and lawyers to protect us. Mr. Sock even has his own office that I'm not allowed into. I have to stand at the door with only my arm inside while he has his secret meetings.

Wait a minute...he just ordered me to give YOU the following message: "Wear a sock puppet on your hand. It's the only way to find out who you truly are, bring peace to planet Earth, and allow all the remaining, delightful, sock life-forms to transfer into our dimension."

I'd listen to him if I were you.

Commentary: Comedy can really backfire sometimes.

MEANING OF LIFE

There was a young man named Josh who had the urge to go out and discover the true meaning of life because he was of short stature and wanted an edge in life to help make him more successful. He was also quite curious about the nature of human consciousness. Through his tireless inquiries he discovered there was a very wise old man that lived at the top of a distant mountain who claimed to have enlightenment.

Josh saved up his money, bought a suitcase, and set off to find this elderly wise guy. Arriving at the bus station early and getting through the many security checkpoints, he traveled for days and days until he arrived at the faraway land. He then found a taxicab to take him to the base of the mountain where he ascended the rest of the way by foot. Weary, wet, and cold, he reached the massive wooden gate at the summit, knocked three times, and was admitted to the castle.

"Why have you come?" questioned the gatekeeper.

"I seek to learn the meaning of life," Josh replied. The gatekeeper explained that he first had to live and work there for five years before being granted an audience to ask one question. So Josh stayed for five long years doing all kinds of menial chores like washing pots and pans, giving piggy-back rides, and taking care of their pet goat, named Rhonda.

Finally the big day arrived, and he was ushered into the Great Hall where the wise man was drinking coffee and listening to *Car Talk* on public radio.

"Oh great and wise one, please tell me the meaning of life and, if you can, the nature of our consciousness."

The old man peered intently at Josh and answered, "Well, dat's two questions. So, I'm tellin' ya, life is like da bean sprout...ain't it? Eh?" and he smiled benevolently.

"What?!" Josh exploded, "Let me get this straight. I

wasted five years to hear you say life is like a bean sprout, and you're not even sure?"

"If ya wants a second opinion," the old man said calmly, "dere's anudder wise man ninety miles west a here on anudder mountain peak. Go ask him if yer such a smarty-pants. Besides, you smell like a goat."

"Damn right I'm going. And thanks for nothing, you schmuck." With that, Josh left and began his journey westward. A month later he arrived at the other peak, wet and cold, and was admitted to the castle but was told he would have to live and work there for five long years before meeting their wise man to ask his one question.

"One thing I want to know first," Josh demanded. "This wise man of yours isn't going to tell me life is like a bean sprout, is he?"

"Beans? Nah, of course not," the gatekeeper laughed. "Ever'body here knows dat life ain't like da bean sprout. Sheesh!" So, with that, Josh was put to work doing all kinds of menial chores like waxing floors, giving piggyback rides, and taking care of their big pet rabbit, named Eric Bartholomew.

Finally the big day arrived, and Josh was ushered into the Great Hall where the old man was drinking hot chocolate and listening to *Fresh Air* on public radio.

"Oh great and wise one, please tell me the meaning of life, and if you can, the nature of our consciousness," Josh implored humbly.

The old man looked him in the eye and answered, "I tells ya, dat's two questions, not one. What was yer name? Never mind. Why do you think annoying strangers is fun? I *was* gonna say dat life is like da lotus flower...ain't it? Heh heh. But, I can tell from the way you're staring at me, kinda scary, that you is smarter than dat, so I will share with you a separate reality, Carlos. Life is like a circus and each of us are bleeping clowns.

"Now get out of here, you smell like a rabbit."

BED-BEARS

Each night, Mom said the same thing as she tucked Mikey into bed with his teddy bear, closed his closet door, and turned out the light.

"Good night, sleep tight; don't let the bed-bears bite." Little Mikey sometimes pondered this as he went to sleep. He had examined his teddy bear closely for teeth, and it had none. He took warnings seriously ever since his recent experiment with a partially inserted electrical plug and a bar magnet, which he discovered on his own without any input from the Internet.

BOOM!

The boy also diligently observed warnings regarding crossing busy streets, touching hot stoves, and especially wondered about that "if I die before I wake" monologue he was forced to repeat. What kind of warning was *that*? He tried hard not to die and was overly aware of his own breathing when he remembered it. He asked his big sister about that saying and she patiently explained it was likely Mom meant he could die unexpectedly at any moment, which scared him even more. Then she taught him "The Hearse Song" (The worms crawl in, the worms crawl out, the worms play pinochle on your snout).

One day at school he discovered the other kids' moms used a similar phrase but it involved bedbugs, not bed-bears. He wasn't afraid of bugs. He stomped on bugs even though Mom was scared of them. She'd scream hysterically upon seeing any size spider, and God only knows what effect that had on the lad as an infant.

Several weeks later, as she was tucking him in, Mom repeated, "Good night, sleep tight; don't let the bed-bears bite." She smiled, gave him a wink, and walked to the window, opened it slightly, and left the room after making sure his closet door was securely closed so the ghost couldn't get out.

After an hour of sleep, little Mikey was awakened by something that bumped his bed. He remained motionless, listening to the sound of heavy breathing and noticing an odor he had never smelled before. It was kind of like damp fur mixed with a hint of…poop. Suddenly, a big wet nose swept across him and snorted, and his mind became gripped with terror. Calling Mom might startle the creature and cause it to attack, he didn't know, so he laid there motionless and rightly assumed this was indeed a real, live bear. The infamous bed-bear! It shuffled through his room, bumping into stuff and sniffing around. Did Mom let it in? Was she still mad at him for snooping through all her dresser drawers?

After a few minutes he heard it lie down; perhaps it was tired. Mikey barely breathed until he believed it was safe and then, remembering the warning, quietly got out of bed and tiptoed gingerly to the door. He turned the knob sooo very slowly, inched the door open, and sprang out, slamming it shut behind him. He heard the bed-bear rise up with a growl and Mikey jumped up and down, waving his arms in panic with a look of alarm on his face.

He ran screaming down the hallway to wake his parents and as he turned the corner to reach their door, he bumped into a big mountain lion that looked as if it had just come out of the bathroom. They both stared silently at each other and after a few brief moments it picked him up in its jaws by the back of his pajamas, carried him through the open front door, and unceremoniously dropped him in the middle of the lawn.

The lion stood there looking down at him, slowly shaking its head. Next, he saw the bear climbing out of his window with his teddy bear in its mouth, and then the bear and the lion ran toward the forest.

"Damn it," Mikey swore to himself, "Mom never warned me about bed-lions!"

LUCKY DAY

Once there was a herd of rabbits that lived happily in the forest. Their main hobby was making lists of items they had seen and how much there was of it so that they knew where everything was (that, and synchronized hopping, which they were hoping would one day be recognized as an Olympic event). Their only enemy was a deranged cow named Ernie who had a voracious appetite for rabbit stew (also called hasenpfeffer).

One day, Honey Bunny was out looking for shallots, garlic, and peppercorns for a recipe when she tripped, fell, and injured her ankle. The others took her to the local animal clinic run by a peculiar porcupine and she was bandaged up. When asked the cost for treatment, the doctor said she was lucky; it would only cost an arm and a leg.

He was kidding, of course, but the rabbits didn't realize that because they had seen so-called Lucky Rabbits' Feet advertised in magazines. They took Honey and ran off without paying, and this annoyed Dr. Timmy considerably. He cursed under his breath for a while and then hired a collection agency to get the three bucks and late fee they owed him. Three dollars is a lot in the animal world, and he was saving up to purchase a steam-powered tongue rotator which a slick, fast-talking medical company representative had convinced him he needed.

The rabbits saw Honey was slow in getting well so they hoped that a group run would be just the thing to encourage healing, help bond the community, and make it easier for some of them to quit smoking. They organized several Poker Runs wherein they would scurry through the forest and keep their lists up to date while trying to make a "full house." They arranged special hosting with local establishments such as the Mosquito Bar, the Road Kill Diner, and Club Bambi which would have decks of playing cards handy for them.

The Poker Runs began and the bunnies ran in single file to hide their true number. One of their paths took them through Turtle Territory but they quit using it once they learned the turtles didn't quite appreciate their presence.

Unbeknownst to the bunnies, Ernie was working for the collection agency Timmy had hired. Ernie was lucky to get the job since his credit was running out at Club Bambi, and he was hiding behind a tree awaiting their arrival during the latest run.

As the lead rabbit approached, Ernie jumped out abruptly and blocked their path, shouting, "Where's the money you owe?" The rabbits were startled and didn't know what to say so they ran in different directions and scampered home to discuss this new turn of events. Various ideas were brought up, such as taking out a loan or working for a living, but each suggestion was worse than the last. They decided to just continue running and hopefully an idea would dawn on them.

Honey Bunny healed nicely, but one day while she was out gathering Arabbita beans for their gourmet coffee, she was confronted by Ernie, who was drunk.

"Where's my money, you little coney?" he growled. (Calling a female rabbit a coney is great insult.)

"I don't have it, Mr. Cow. I'm sorry. None of us have any money," she said fearfully, and then had a flash of inspiration. "I am good at riddles if you'd like to play for the money, double or nothing."

"All right, runny-babbit, I'm smarter than you any day of the week. What is your riddle?"

"Tell me, what is alive without breath, as cold as death, never thirsty, ever drinking, all in mail, never clinking," Honey recited.

"That's easy," said the cow. "It's a mailman in winter. No, wait, it's a cold beer."

"Is that your final answer?" she asked.

"No," yelled the cow. "It's a cold, drunken, zombie mailman. Ha! I got it! You owe me double now."

"You're wrong," the rabbit replied timidly, "The correct answer is a fish. Think about it." Ernie got steaming mad and barked ferociously and Honey ran.

She dutifully deliberated on how to pay her medical bill. After all, Honey was an honest bunny and never took things that didn't belong to her, except a pen now and then, but the cow was not playing fair. True, she owed a debt, but she had won the bet with Ernie so it was easy to justify her subsequent action.

Late that evening, Honey bravely went alone to the van down by the river where Ernie lived and, while he slept, removed his gold pendant from the antler coat-rack tied to the side view mirror. She brought it to the doctor's office the next day in payment and demanded change, for it was worth at least ten dollars. All she got back was a pile of raw copper and zinc.

She stood there staring at it for a long time until Timmy stated, "OK Honey, I can see that that ain't gonna work out, so I'll tell ya what I'm gonna do. For the next month, free prostate and pelvic exams for your entire frickin' herd. I'll even make house calls. Yup, this is yer lucky day."

TWISTER

I vividly recall that gloomy, early evening when the clouds were ominously green and swirling like the proverbial frog in a blender. It felt like the mother of all storms was about to unleash her fury upon us. The storm siren wailed like a tortured spirit, and we totally freaked out as a huge funnel dropped from the sky, ravaging the ground and thundering like a freight train.

Ma screamed for everyone to run to the basement, like immediately, but something about the scene drew us in as if we were hypnotized by the otherworldliness of it all. It repelled and attracted us at the same time so we simply stood there, watching.

Sarah was the first to be lifted and carried away, then Ellen and little Billy, and lastly it pried Ma's bony fingers from the railing. Luckily for me, I had tied my legs with the garden hose so I kind of floated and bobbed like some demented kite until the worst of it was over. It was an experience I shall never forget because I had blades of grass impacted up my nose.

After I sneezed several times and calmed down, I looked for my family, but to no avail. For all I know, they were blown clear to Oz and our belongings scattered to the four corners of the earth. That night I curled up to sleep in the bathtub since the plumbing was still intact.

The next day, I saw a guy walking around with a sock puppet on his hand trying to cheer people up. He gave the distinct impression that he'd taken a severe blow to the head and might be suffering from toxic sock syndrome. My appeals to the authorities for help went unheeded as they were too busy with another search.

Crews were scouring the remains of the high school which had taken the brunt of the tornado in the midst of their annual spring performance (something lame about Goldilocks).

My family and I would have been there had I not been rejected for a part in the musical. I was looking for a small role, that's all, it's not like I wanted to be the star or anything. I had hoped I could play the wolf or one of its friends.

The audition for the show began as a very boring experience. After standing around for*ever* with a bunch of other kids, I thought it would be amusing to howl like a wolf. I am good at howling and can always get the neighborhood dogs started. The students around me were laughing, and some of them howled also. After a while the drama coach got irritated and I was given a simple choice: behave or get out. Of course, that took all the fun out of it. After a few more tiny test howls, yelps really, the other kids gave me dirty looks as well.

Well, who did they think they were? I howled and howled all the more to teach them the lesson that I have the right to audition in my own unique way, which lasted until the music director grabbed my arm and personally escorted me from the room. I'm sure everyone was howling with laughter behind my back.

So what if I can't be in their stupid musical? I think they should have been nicer to me. Obviously these people have no sense of humor and don't belong in show biz. They totally pissed me off, those big idiots.

Hell, I'm mad at the whole stupid school now...I never liked it there anyway...if I could have caused a giant twister to come and smash it all, I would have!

Turns out God did it for me.
Thanks, God.

Big Idiots

Once there was a family of not-too-bright raccoons that lived under an abandoned shed near the outskirts of a sleepy little village, and they had a fairly decent life. Their hobbies included stargazing and grooming, but they especially loved to dine and considered themselves gourmets. (One of their favorite recipes called for adding a can of peas to the tuna helper.) What they liked most was raiding the garden of old Mr. Gregorian which had lots of nice juicy vegetables.

However, Mr. Gregorian confronted them one warm July evening while they were feasting and laid down the law. He made it abundantly clear that they were no longer welcome by throwing firecrackers at them, hurting their tiny ears and forcing them to flee.

Back at the shed, the coons sat and discussed what had gone wrong. Old Papa raccoon stated his opinion that Mr. Gregorian must be a big idiot not to allow such sweet raccoons as themselves to eat in his garden, and perhaps they should leave that spot alone.

The younger ones now assumed Papa was a weak leader and maybe even a big idiot himself, and one of them should challenge him for his leadership position. So the strongest, named Robert, did just that and actually won after a noisy, protracted battle which ended when he kicked the old man in the coconuts. Papa was allowed to remain but could not make any group decisions as they were now certain he was a big idiot, and because his voice had become an octave higher.

A few days later, they returned to Mr. Gregorian's patch without Papa and feasted anew, hoping the old man had forgotten about them after such a long absence. He hadn't. He ran out, lit a couple of really big firecrackers, and tossed them into their midst, which hurt their tiny ears and caused a general panic. They scrambled home and once more sat and discussed what had gone wrong.

Of course, Papa was there to say, "I told you so." Robert had to keep up appearances and not let them think he was a big idiot also, so he told them he had a plan. He declared he would go alone to Mr. Gregorian the next day and negotiate a treaty wherein they could gain access to what they wanted in exchange for certain favors. Robert did not say what those favors were, but his backup plan involved a well-placed kick to a big idiot.

The following day, Mr. Gregorian saw him coming and had ready a disguised cage containing carrots. The raccoon could not resist so he walked in and started eating, yum! A string was pulled, a gate fell, and Mr. Gregorian won the next round. Robert protested and offered his favors but since he didn't speak English, it was an exercise in futility. Mr. G was singing strangely to himself as he drove the raccoon into the forest and unceremoniously dumped him in unknown territory.

Late that evening, the others wondered where Robert was and chose to let Papa be leader again since the swelling had gone down. Papa steered them away from Mr. Gregorian's garden, and instead they raided a dumpster at a nearby fast food joint, yum! They took their spoil to the warm, dark, empty street for their feast and while eating, pointed out to each other the Summer Triangle stars up in the sky. Ten minutes later, some drunken clowns in a Jeep came zooming along and carelessly flattened several of them, including Papa.

Eventually Robert returned and took the survivors down the road less traveled by into the woods to live, and that made all the difference. As they reflected on the meaning of life, it was concluded in their wisdom that while raccoons are imperfect beasts, human beings are perfect beasts.

GOING TO THE AIRPORT

Little Mikey often wished he was an only child, especially when his older sister teased him and made him mad. Life sure was frustrating when he didn't get his way. Mom and Dad always sided with her, and she had a way of making his bad decisions look like they were always his fault. Sometimes his life seemed existentially meaningless but when he was having fun, it was glorious.

One summer afternoon, as he was playing with his plastic army men in the front yard, a light-blue Ford Mustang drove up slowly and parked at his curb. A voice called to him so sweetly that he stopped playing and glanced up. The young lady in the car was dressed in a brown, vintage-style dress from the 1940s and had shoulder-length auburn hair, light blue eyes, and a friendly smile. He approached the car cautiously since his parents had warned him about talking to strangers, but this one time should be OK.

Leaning across the passenger seat she said to him, "Hello son, my name is Susan."

"I'm not your son," he responded. "And what's a classy dame like you doing in this neck of the woods?"

"I'm on my way to the airport and seem to have become lost. Can you direct me?" That caught his interest because he liked watching the jets flying overhead, some with long, puffy white tails. According to Dad, the tails contained chemicals designed to make brothers and sisters get along together, but they sure didn't work on sisters.

"No ma'am," he replied, "I can't. I'm just a kid."

Her eyes looked disappointed but she smiled, waved for him to come closer, and continued, "Say, I could use a little companionship, would you like to tag along? I have an extra ticket."

He was tempted but knew he would be in a world of trouble if he did, so he regarded her quizzically and inquired, "Izzat so? Where are you flying to?"

"To the Land of the Magic Love Crickets, of course," she answered. His eyes widened with interest and he felt a tingle run down his spine.

"Gee, that sounds like a swell place. What's it like?" She gave him a bigger smile and motioned him to come closer still.

"It's a land of green fields and blue skies where you ride on giant butterflies, see? You get to eat ice cream whenever you want, play the electric synthesizer, and never have to go to school. I have some of the magic crickets here in this shoebox, would you like to hold one?" She removed the lid, exposing the writhing dirt within, and threw her voice like a ventriloquist to imitate faint voices calling from the box.

Mikey was leaning through the window to look when she grabbed him by the collar and slapped a dab of enchanted tar on his head. His innocent little cry of "Say, what's the big ideaaa?" went unnoticed as he shriveled and shrank and in less than five seconds had turned into a cricket himself. She looked around cautiously and let out a giggle as she put him into the box and replaced the lid. She would love him just like all the others.

Susan peered down the street and observed more children playing in their front yards.

"It sure is taking a long time to get to the airport," she said to herself.

Commentary: If you think this is funny, you are probably a potential psychopath like me.

CLOUD ALPHABET

Ever since I was a kid I've enjoyed looking at clouds and the shapes they seem to present – animals, faces, and all sorts of phantasmagorical images that slowly change with the wind. I'd like to be able to spend an entire week on the roof watching clouds and taking pictures of the really remarkable ones, which I could put in a book and sell to other people who think that unique-looking clouds are interesting.

Recently I came up with the idea of forming a cloud alphabet. What if certain cloud shapes could be made to represent letters of our alphabet so that on any given day, you or I could look up and see words spelled out in the sky? What would they say to us?

For fun, I sketched out fifty general shapes and assigned a letter or number (0-9) to each one. Letters that are used more often, like E and T, were represented more than once. I used only the fluffy cumulus clouds and not the flat gray stratus that covers the entire sky. It took a long time to do this as they kept changing shapes and I don't draw too well. Nevertheless, I was eager to see what the sky had to say, if anything.

On the first morning after the project was completed I went outside, gazed upward, and saw the words "sta hoom," so I called in sick to work. I went outside two hours later to see if there was more and, to my dismay, three clouds had formed the letters LOL, which can mean "laughing out loud" as well as "lots of luck" and "loads of laundry." Was the sky laughing at me? I went in and checked the laundry bin to see if it was full. It wasn't.

I went out later to see what else might be up there and decoded a series of numbers scattered about, which I interpreted to mean I should play those lucky numbers in the lottery. I drove to the gas station, played them in differing combinations, and came home in the hope of becoming rich beyond the wildest dreams of avarice. Unfortunately, every ticket lost. I wondered if there was intelligence behind these messages. Was I being too subjective? For the most part the letters and numbers were random and formed no words at all.

The next morning was a clear blue sky with no clouds, so I was being ignored.

The morning after that, as I was getting into my car, I saw the word "krash" so naturally I stayed home and called in sick again. It turned out later that afternoon a neighbor lady had been driving on the expressway, had slammed on the brakes to miss a stray dog, and caused a dump truck behind her to have to suddenly swerve and drive into the median, tip over, and land on its side. I guess the message had been for the guy in the truck and I felt confused. How in the world was I to know which messages were for me and which weren't?

The next morning, I didn't look up at all. I ran out, got in my car, put it in gear, and fed gas. I'd already missed too many days and I needed that temp job. As I drove, I couldn't help but notice that the sky was now saying words I didn't understand at all, such as "estupido." Who knows what *that* means?

As I walked into the building I took a last look at the sky and saw the words "up yers," right before it started raining. I slammed the door, went to my workstation, and tore up the drawings I had made.

I no longer think a cloud alphabet is a good idea because we have a rude, immature sky!

THE APPLE BAPPLE

Once there was an apple named Annie Bapple who was the proudest apple on the tree. There in the orchard life was good and the days were long, and she got bigger and redder than everyone else. Of course, the others resented her and made comments like, "So, who the hell does she think *she* is?" and "Why I oughta...."

One day in late September, workers came and put Annie in a bushel basket along with the other apples from her tree. They all jostled into each other and many took a jab at Annie with their stems. She screamed that it wasn't fair but the humans didn't hear her, so she bounced out of the basket and set off to find fame and fortune clad only in her red leotard.

As she was traveling, she encountered a strange old fox that offered to give her directions to the big city. The fox had shifty eyes and acted unusually friendly, which aroused her suspicions. Taking her leave with thanks, Annie noticed herself being followed but she outsmarted the fox by pretending to be an angry red bird, and continued on alone.

An hour later, she met a young Brussels sprout that had more in common with Annie than she would admit. The sprout was proud and boastful and full of unrealistic ideas. After a brief conversation, she could tell it really wanted to be her friend so she ran off. (She was bad at relationships that lasted more than twenty minutes.)

Annie rolled along the side of the road until she came to a busy intersection that she attempted to navigate several times, but had to hurry back each time after almost becoming applesauce. Some clown in a Jeep swerved to try to hit her on purpose and nearly made her crap herself!

While waiting for an opportunity to cross over, she chanced to strike up a conversation with a friendly old peddler named Brogan who was quite knowledgeable about apples, and who offered to help her get to the other side. Annie jumped into his pouch and settled down, expecting to be let out soon but the peddler didn't open the pouch until he was at his roadside stand. He took Annie and set her in a display container, face down, with a price sticker across her butt.

Annie became angry at him and yelled and threatened using *very* bad language. Brogan soon grew annoyed with her insults so he picked her up and shook her violently. This made Annie dizzy and even madder so she stabbed at him with her stem. In a fit of fury, the peddler took a bite out of her hide and hurled "Her Royal Fruitiness" far into the bushes. He instantly regretted his loss of temper, but it was too late.

Annie Bapple sat there awhile, feeling injured and alone, and then cried her eyes out. She felt her life was over and she would never get to do the things she longed for, such as touring with the Rolling Stones or receiving a lifetime achievement award from the Royal Astronomical Society.

Annie's body slowly turned brown as the insects took notice. It wasn't long before a steady stream of bugs helped themselves to her sweetness until there was nothing left except her stem, brown seeds, and some embarrassing cartilage. She now dearly wished she had befriended the Brussels sprout.

Life is like that sometimes. Grow up and deal with it already.

PINCHY THE CRAB

There once was a red crab named Pinchy who lived alone in the ocean, not so much by choice but by direct request of his fellow Reds. Pinchy assumed the other crabs were envious of him because he played the harmonica and could read Basic English.

Pinchy put his heart into his "harp" but had been born with only a modicum of musical talent, so his playing usually sounded like cats giving birth on a speeding freight train. But, and this is the point, at least he tried and screw what the other crabs thought. They were clicking idiots in his opinion.

One day, as he was sitting in his crab shack, a slimy pocket dictionary floated down from above.

"Click, This must be a gift from the gods," he clicked softly to himself. He was delighted with his new find and studied the book to the best of his limited ability. Pinchy discovered a world of newfangled words which he then used in making other crabs feel inferior by his fancy clicking and by making fun of their names whenever he went into town to shop, do laundry, or visit his sick cousin, Spongiform Bob.

He was fond of interrupting others with, "Click, Shut up, I'm smarter than you are," when someone else was clicking. But sometimes Pinchy would click a new word, such as "smaragdine," that he did not understand, and one could tell he had no clue of what he had just clicked.

A couple of weeks later, a mean old crab named Buster told him in front of a large gathering of marine creatures, "Click, Pinchy, you're simply pretending to be smart. You click as poorly as you play that stupid harmonica. And, if you want a second opinion, you're ugly." Then while everyone was laughing, Buster kicked him squarely in the pants.

Poor Pinchy was hurt and humiliated. He took his

harmonica and skittered away, taking the very long path back to his burrow. He whimpered along the way because he felt he did not fit in anywhere in their stupid society, and then played some agonizing blues on his harmonica.

Meanwhile, some of the crabs went and ransacked his home, taking special delight in shredding his dictionary. Never again would Pinchy find new words from this book to click fun at their names or make them feel like ragged claws scuttling across the floors of silent seas. They would once more be able to express themselves naturally without fear of being mocked. Incidentally, they also found a nude picture of an eel named Eliot hidden under his mattress. Shocking.

After they were through fiddling around in his cave, they heard the distant sound of...bad harmonica music. Pinchy was returning home. The crabs slapped themselves on their foreheads and moaned "Click click click click," which I think is crab language for "Oh crap!"

The herd of crabs clickly suggested ideas to get rid of Pinchy once and for all, many of which revolved around using their pincers to crush his harmonica, and shoving him into one of those cages that dropped down from time to time from above.

However, before they could take action, Pinchy saw that his crab cottage was crammed with crustaceans and changed course, this time heading downstream with the ocean current accompanied by floating bits and pieces of his smaragdine dictionary.

"That'll teach you to play the blues and learn to read!" they all clicked loudly after him.

Commentary: Nobody likes not being part of the clique.

Making New Friends

I've found a great new way of making friends which is better than my usual method of staring at strangers to see if they will notice me and say something. It doesn't cost much, and these friends remain loyal for weeks. Here is the secret: you buy helium-filled balloons, take them home, and draw a face on each one (and perhaps write their name on the back of their head). You can also draw on their naughty parts but never invite real people over to see them like that; it violates some privacy law and can give you an unwanted reputation. Anyway, they might be male or female, plain or fancy; it's up to you to choose exactly what your friends will look like.

The next thing to do is attach the proper weight to each so they float at nearly eye level. They will, of course, bob up and down and move depending on the air currents. Make sure you keep them away from open doors and windows so they can't willingly escape.

Balloon people will take on personalities of their own, and are a lot like real people. For instance, two of my old balloon buddies invested in a silver mine but went bust. Ms. Kayan was a long, thin balloon who got twisted out of shape and believed she was a giraffe. One named Howard wanted to be a DJ and was full of hot air, and another named Barb inspired fear in the others.

In fact, I have several here with me as I write this. Mr. Montgolfier is hovering next to the computer and his cousin, Gregory the Mediocre, recently floated around the corner to inspect the dining room. By the far wall near the window are Marsha, Jan, and Cindy Windy.

We have wonderful conversations on a wide variety of topics. I have found that each balloon person is at least as smart as I am, although they do have the annoying habit of drifting away unpredictably during a talk. They are not very good at keeping eye contact but they more than compensate for it by being great listeners. Balloon folks never need to use the bathroom and won't raid the refrigerator while I'm asleep. Also, they're good sports about taking a punch to the head.

The depressing fact is that these friends have very short lives. It becomes evident they are near the end when they've fallen and can't get up, even with their weight and string removed. Most of them face death with dignity and are resigned to their fate. They receive comfort as I assure them that one day I will travel the same road, but in a different fashion since I am not filled with helium. I've already lost many friends this way. Incidentally, after a few days I take their lifeless corpse outside when the others aren't looking and compassionately shoot a BB between their eyes then toss the carcass in the trash – so sad. (Not my first choice, but the guy at the funeral home told me to go away or he'd call the cops.)

Balloon friends love to watch television. I have an old tube TV and with the static on the screen, they will remain glued there for hours. Confrontational daytime talk shows are their favorites. You should also know they are deathly afraid of open flames and jagged edges. Balloon people appreciate classical music and fine paintings but are not fond of pop art. Get the point? I'm sure you do, but I couldn't resist the pun. I like to think I have a sharp wit, but don't needle me about it.

It looks like Greg returned and chased Jan and Cindy away. Now he and Marsha are having a romantic interlude by the bookshelf; I guess I'll leave them alone for a while. I'm not worried about Marsha getting pregnant because her tube is tied.

So remember, if you need friends like I do, think "balloon people."

ALL GROWN UP

Scooter and Biff lived far away in a sleepy little village and were brothers and best friends. In the foothills of the Mystee mountain was an old abandoned sawmill where they went exploring, although Mother had forbidden it. The place hadn't been in use for over one hundred and fifty years, the timbers were rotting, and it was overrun with ferns, weeds, and nameless critters whose eyes gleamed in the setting sun. Scooter and Biff would play hide and seek, dig for treasure, and use it as their fort. It was a rickety old dump, but it was theirs.

The boys often felt that life was moving too slowly. So many rules and restrictions made the 10 and 11 year-olds want to grow up faster and have the freedom they saw others having on television.

One summer evening, while watching an old Humphrey Bogart movie, Scooter had a brainstorm. What makes children grow into adults? Obviously, it was cigarettes! Mom smoked like a chimney, so one evening after dinner they stole a cigarette and a small box of wooden matches from her purse and hurried excitedly to the mill to have a smoke. This would make them feel all grown up, they were sure.

Scooter took the cigarette and lit it, puffing carefully at the tip, then took a deep drag. The hot smoke entered his lungs and instantly caused him to cough in uncontrollable spasms. Biff got jealous and took a hit for himself, with the same result. So there they were, all grown up and coughing like they had just inhaled shredded tree bark.

In fact, they coughed so long and loud that they awoke the skeleton ghost that was buried deep in the cellar. The ghostly skull gazed around angrily and then realized where the disturbance was coming from. Children! The old skeleton ghost disliked children intensely due to its own unresolved negative emotions stemming from childhood issues involving trust (some kids had once kicked over his sandcastle and laughed. It's a seemingly endless cycle).

Mr. Ghost preferred to sleep all day, get up after sundown, and hang around the mill all alone while remembering the good old days when it had the joy of turning live trees into lumber. It bared its teeth, growled, and floated up to stalk the noisy intruders.

In the dim twilight Scooter saw it first, hovering in midair: a bleached-bone skeleton with empty eye sockets glowing dull red and patches of skin like translucent parchment stretched across parts of its decayed, bony body. Its evil grin went right through to Scooter's soul.

"Yikes!" he shrieked, and bolted toward the exit, dropping the cigarette. Biff turned, saw the ghost, and followed screaming on Scooter's heels. The youngsters ran in terror without looking back until they were safely home. Both of them vowed never to go there again and instead of smoking, agreed to learn to play poker. That would make them feel all grown up, they were sure.

After midnight, the spectral creature ventured forth to visit the boys and teach them a lesson. It materialized under each of their beds in turn with a big pouch of slimy cigarette butts and spread them on the floor. Then it wailed like a banshee while tipping over their beds, and vanished. When Mother rushed in and saw the mess, the boys were in a heap of trouble and got grounded for two whole weeks.

The ghost floated back to the sawmill laughing its fool head off (and putting it on again) then finished smoking the cigarette the boys had dropped.

It was a very grown-up ghost.

MOVIE THEATER

I usually avoid movie theaters, especially the first few weeks after a new film is released because I don't like being in big crowds. I prefer to attend when the show has been out for over a month so that most people have seen it and stay away, but even then it's a gamble on the annoyances that can occur. Many times it's best to skip the theater altogether and simply wait for the DVD release.

When there are too many people in one place they seem to lose responsibility for their actions and become rude. They act thoughtlessly by talking, bumping your seat, using cell-phones, and occasionally spilling food and drinks. Some folks totally ignore you when you ask them to show a little consideration. Still, I like the rare movie premier as much as the next person (if the next person dislikes crowded theaters) so I thought I'd design a special movie-premier-watching suit to help me feel more comfortable in the multitude.

I started with high-grade Kevlar armor that I bought from local teenagers and made a body cast that I could step into and seal, with a helmet made of the same. I installed internal hydraulic motors to the body in order to add strength to my arms and legs, and gave the helmet a bulletproof visor. I also added a catheter but you probably don't need to know that. For once, I was able to create something that didn't require aluminum foil. Finally, I added a cape that I cut from one of my girlfriend's black satin sheets (please don't tell her) and I was ready.

Standing in the ticket line I got several envious looks, but that's to be expected. I bought a small bag of popcorn then went in and found a seat, only to discover that there was no way to get the popcorn into my mouth through the visor so I "accidentally" dropped the bag on the floor. Since this was a first release, the place became jam-packed very quickly and it looked like every seat was taken.

Eventually the lights dimmed and after another twenty minutes of stupid commercials and previews, the movie began.

Everything was going well until the young adults behind me talked loudly when they weren't supposed to, so I turned around and said, "Shhhhhhhhh!!" One told me to do something to myself that I wasn't in the mood to do. I was thinking they had probably smoked a white, rock-like substance before coming in, when one of them bumped my seat. I assumed it was an accident, but when it happened again four minutes later I impulsively stood up, hopped over my chair, and grabbed two of those boneheads by their shirts.

Using my new strength, I sent one guy flying headfirst into the aisle and forcefully directed my knee into the other guy's private parts. People booed me, several cheered, so I politely yelled at them all to shut the hell up and watch the movie, and I kindly sat down. A short time later, an obnoxious little old lady came by with an usher and I was asked to leave.

Heck with that, I paid to get in and I wasn't causing any trouble so I totally ignored them. The old woman fished in her bag, pulled out a potted fern, and hurled it at my helmet while calling me a dork, and left. Ten minutes later the police arrived and they requested I leave, even though I explained I was simply trying to watch the picture in peace.

Suddenly, the movie screen went dark and the house lights came up. Oh well, I guess this show was ending early for some odd reason. I exited with several police hanging on me and one dragging from my leg but I was unstoppable. Unfortunately, my cool cape got torn off in the process. Once outside, I leaped away and there was nothing they could do about it. Later on, after I had removed the suit, I returned for my car.

See why I like DVDs better than movie theaters? No stupid commercials and previews!

Dancing With Matches

There was a very clever fox that lived in the Mystee forest where people never party till sunrise or drink so much that they get sick. Well…hardly ever…OK, some of the time. His name is of no consequence, but you know it nonetheless for he is Everett Everyfox, and his "tail" is timeless.

So anyway, Mr. Everyfox was prowling around one evening looking for discarded beer bottles when, in a small clearing lit by moonlight, he spied eight tiny, bearded gnomes doing a peculiar dance around a small box of wooden matches. The gnome named Theodore had seen a young human make fire from it. Shortly thereafter, he saw two of them run off screaming and leave it behind. Now, the box and all the power it contained belonged to the gnomes, whether for good or evil.

Everett was determined to investigate this since he was hungry and curious, and everyone knows foxes love to eat magical gnomes since foxes are immune to magic. (If you didn't know that, you do now.) He approached quietly under cover and soon was close enough to jump out and catch one. However, he remained mesmerized by their antics.

Fred, the president-elect of the gnomes, soon realized that dancing was not making anything happen to the box so they stopped to confer. One suggested singing instead of dancing, but their goofy songs held no sway with the matchbox either. It was finally agreed that they should just open the darn thing. Doing that, they gazed awestruck upon the red-tipped sticks inside and, after silly-dancing around those for several minutes and singing the safety warning, Fred removed one and held it high.

"We are blessed this night," he exclaimed. "We have power undreamed of! What shall we gnomes do with this magnificent gift?" They all shouted excitedly that the box of matches should be enshrined so that other magical gnomes could visit it and they would grow rich from tourism. Fred announced they would do exactly that, but test one first to see if it really did create fire. After all, he reasoned, they must have proof. That's how legends are made. No gnome is going to embark upon a long journey to see a box of what might be useless twigs solely based on hearsay.

Fred figured they might get one goblin-dollar from each visitor, maybe more in the beginning before the novelty wore thin. If they could invent a way to tie it mystically to their heritage, they could hopefully make it a requirement that every adult gnome had to undertake a pilgrimage to it on a yearly basis. That would allow Fred and his faithful following to start investing in restaurants and hotel construction.

They were about to strike the match against the box when Everett pounced and caught the one in the tall yellow hat, named Alvin, in his mouth. The others scattered clumsily into the night.

"They run like drunken ducks," the fox thought, and chuckled to himself. Alvin avowed that he was not ready to die yet as he had not compiled a list of his good works to show God, and asked for a chance to find someone to accompany him to the next world as a character witness. Everett jumped at the chance to eat two of them, but Alvin could not find anyone willing to join in his folly, and was subsequently devoured in one big gulp.

The next day, the remaining gnomes assembled, struck the match, and burned down a large section of forest to teach that fox a lesson (which immediately became a major part of their heritage). This lesson might also apply to people around here who party and drink too much.

Never mess around with dancing magical gnomes who have matches!

A Turn at the Wheel

While Scooter and Biff were spending a summer vacation at their grandmother's house in the city, they were pleasantly surprised one day by the arrival of a big cardboard box at the curb. A neighbor had discarded it after an appliance delivery, and the boys dragged it to their backyard and covered it with a blue plastic tarp. Then they got busy furnishing the inside with a variety of sensors and controls created from construction paper and magic markers.

The box held mystery, adventure, and a miniaturized universe for them to explore. Scooter and Biff became intergalactic grasshoppers, deranged bounty hunters, soldiers of fortune, temporary security guards, time travelers, and insomniac truckers. They knew all and sensed all yet were still open to wonder and amazement.

One beautiful afternoon, Scooter and Biff left their box at grandmother's insistence and went to the neighborhood park to play on the shiny new playground equipment which the city had recently installed after a long delay due to insurance and legal concerns. There were swings that sat on the ground, slides with no stairs, and the monkey bar. At the bar sat three unemployed monkeys, each with a warm, stale glass of Old Warthog beer. They eyed Scooter and Biff warily as the pair approached.

The city hadn't anticipated a literal monkey bar, but the zoning petition and plans for the playground had been pushed through committee without proper oversight. It was a powder keg waiting for an ambitious, independent reporter to ignite (but they were few and far between).

Birds were singing in the trees that were swaying in the breeze, and mud was bubbling up in the center of the fountain. Cars zoomed by on the street, planes roared overhead, and 18-wheelers thundered nearby. A sunny blue sky gave warmth to the earth and life seemed good.

Scooter took Biff's baseball cap and threw it up into a tree. Biff grabbed Scooter's shoe and tossed it in the mud. Then, laughing, each one grabbed a drunken monkey by the tail and swung them at each other in a bizarre kind of duel.

After they got that out of their systems, they went to that big wheel that spins around, where you run to get it going then jump onto it and spin until it stops. (What the heck is that thing called? It always made me nauseous.)

They took turns getting it turning and riding but Scooter wanted to make it go fast, real fast, so he said to Biff, "Get back on, I want another turn at the wheel." Biff obliged, and the wheel went so fast that he fell off and hit the dirt while flying sideways. Biff was dizzy and slow getting up, and the monkeys laughed like mad and mocked him.

"I will not be mocked!" Biff yelled angrily.

"Relax, buddy," said Scooter, turning his back on the monkeys and laughing. "You looked funny flying off like that."

Biff took a deep breath and answered, "OK. Now *you* get on, I want another turn at the wheel." Around and around they went, trying to cause each other to fly off into the dirt until grandmother called them for dinner. And there was their box, waiting for them.

I have absolutely no idea where this is leading. I think the box represents imagination, the monkeys are old age, the playground symbolizes the angst of growing up, and the wheel is indicative of time. City government probably represents death.

ALIEN PROBING

I'd had a day like any other, looking for my ideal job online, relaxing in front of the TV with a beer, wondering what is signified by this experience we call life, and then to bed after the news...popped a couple of sleeping pills to help me doze off.

It was around 3:00 a.m. when something made me wake up, but I wasn't totally awake, simply sort of in-between. I tried to move but found myself paralyzed, and panic set in. Suddenly, I sensed an unearthly presence nearby. Forcing open one eye, I saw them standing at my bedside: three silent, gray aliens with big bald heads and large black eyes, sort of reptilian in appearance. After about a minute of staring at me, the short stocky one started to giggle and the tall boney one smacked him hard on the back of his head. My anxiety spiked off the chart but their thoughts permeated my mind and soothed me.

I blacked out and awoke aboard their Stellar-ship. It appeared through the porthole that we were heading for the dark side of the moon, but the ship was flying erratically and it seemed like the pilot was stoned off his ass. I glanced at his name badge and learned he was called Ummagumma. He was doing such a lousy job that I attempted to take the helm and fly it myself since it looked like fun, but he didn't appreciate that one single bit. The next thing I remember, I was on a cold metal table with bright lights overhead, wearing nothing but a white sheet and an embarrassed look on my face.

"We have come to probe you..." their leader, Floyd, droned in a tinny voice, "for information. We seek to learn how to approach and converse with Earth women." I breathed a sigh of relief...but why me? I'm no Romeo. Due to the fact they had probably come millions of light-years for advice, I thought I might as well try to be helpful. Then I thought, wait a minute, I don't owe them anything, and they'll probably probe me where the sun don't shine before they let me go. Therefore, I'll mislead them for the fun of it.

"The first thing you do is walk right up to one and start talking, no matter what she is doing. You want her to know you have confidence," I began.

"A woman will love it when you stare at her, if you know what I mean. Feel free to interrupt when she's talking, and once in a while wink and make a noise like a motorboat. Brag about your extra brain capacity, she'll enjoy that. Talk loudly about your spaceship and how fast it goes. Act like you have things to hide, and never talk about your true feelings. And don't laugh or she will think you're mocking her. Later on, find stuff to criticize. If you run out of things to say, pretend you're a penguin."

I also informed them that they didn't need to bathe, wash their hands, or brush their teeth, if they had any teeth. Since they all wore the same shiny aluminum foil suits, fashion advice didn't seem important. Nevertheless, I informed them that plaid golf pants were the height of fashion nowadays. I went on and on, giving them the worst advice I could think of, and they took it all seriously. One of them was even scribbling down notes.

Stupid aliens.

I must admit they were very respectful the whole time I spoke, and, when I had finished, they thoroughly probed my other end and returned me to my bed. Seriously, why do they do that? Do they want to know what I had for dinner? Is it part of the contract for leasing their ship? What's really happening with them on a deeper level?

So ladies, be on your guard. They're probably out there disguised as guys looking for dates and wearing plaid golf pants. A big clue will be their bad manners.

I want to report this to the police but I know if I tell anyone what happened, I'll be the butt of endless jokes for the rest of my questioning life.

Too Small

There once was a beetle named Brent Idae, nicknamed Buzzy, who lived in a field of tall grass and weeds and who was never guilty of unrestrained emotional outbursts or of being rude at movie theaters. He behaved himself like a good beetle should, but foolishly enjoyed making funny faces at the spiders that lived nearby. He was careful to run when a spider came his way but other than that, life was grand though things can change without warning.

Cricket song floated on the fragrant, midsummer's night air when suddenly the calm, dreamy atmosphere was shattered by such a sound that all the bugs jumped in surprise and looked to see what the matter was. Some clowns were racing their Jeep through the meadow for cheap thrills. All the bugs scampered for their holes or whatever shelter they could find, but several were in the wrong place at the wrong time and got squashed.

It was not pretty.

Buzzy shouted in bug language the equivalent of "Oh crap!" and climbed the nearest dandelion to get a better view of the situation. The Jeep, high beams on, was about one hundred yards from him and coming his way. Blinded by the light, he knew it would find him, he just knew it, and so he sat there waiting for the last possible moment to calculate which direction was the best to leap to safety.

As the growling vehicle approached he felt the thrill of excitement run through his nervous system. He was so caught up in it all that he didn't notice a spider named Puck attach a tiny thread to his back. The Jeep was almost upon him now and as Buzz went to jump to the right, he found he couldn't move. The shock of realization hit him like a brick. Well, maybe not a brick, perhaps more like a tiny pebble falling from a few centimeters above and bouncing off his head, but never mind that part.

Trying not to panic, Buzzy squirmed and strained, but to no avail. The Jeep came crashing through, directly above him now and as it passed, Puck quickly attached a bigger piece of web to *it*. The vehicle ripped the spider along in its wake, with the beetle being sling-shotted up in the air, coming free, and landing on a patch of soft grass.

Buzzy could smell exhaust and caught a whiff of Old Warthog beer as he watched the taillights zigzagging back and forth away from him. He looked around in shock and relief, and then walked to the local bug tavern called The Mosquito Bar where he drank three glasses of sweet cherry wine to steady his nerves and take the sting out of his experience.

Coming out later into the still of the night, he launched into a clever song and dance about how great it is to be a beetle with a girlfriend and a permanent job. Buzzy went home, got into bed, and dreamed of musical blue turtles. His girlfriend smelled the wine on his breath and got up to sleep on the couch. The course of true love never did run smooth.

As for Puck the spider, it pulled itself up onto the Jeep and, finding it inedible, climbed higher and bit one of the occupants who later developed a rash.

The last thought going through Puck's mind as he was being squashed was, "Lord, what fools these mortals be."

Obviously, the spider was too small to actually kill and eat any of them. Why can't we have bigger spiders around here?

THE SEARCH

I had been out partying late that summer night in the big city. I don't drive downtown too often, but ever since I accidentally barfed in a bus driver's fare box after a night of drinking, I'm not allowed on public transportation.

I parked my old Gremlin car and was walking down the avenue to buy some munchies. While passing a dark alley, I saw a brilliant flash of light come from its depths and I stopped for a look. To my surprise, there appeared a giant glowing ball, seven feet tall, with a man and woman stepping out of it. When they were clear, the woman pressed a button, the door closed, and a shiny compact disc came out, which she put in her purse. The giant ball dimmed in brightness and soon became unnoticeable. Dressed in silver pantsuits, the pair walked to the street before going in opposite directions.

She gave me a smile, and, being the gentleman I am, I said, "Excuse me, can I ask what just happened there?"

She held my gaze and gave me a look as if to say, "You'll see, my handsome new friend."

After a few minutes of following her down the street at a discrete distance, a raggedy, middle-aged woman sprang out of a dark doorway, snatched the purse, and ran with it. The woman in silver took off in pursuit with me racing behind them.

The chase ended down another alley in a crowd of homeless people. The woman in silver demanded her purse back, and when the scraggly woman saw that it only contained a disc, she made a bargain; she would trade the purse for the shiny boots the woman was wearing. It was agreed, and the woman in silver got her purse back.

As we were leaving the alley, they were all fighting over the boots. I asked the Silver Lady what the deal was with the disc and everything but she simply looked me in the eye for several moments and smiled, so I followed as she went from store to store looking for something, I knew not what.

Twenty minutes later, the lady in silver started back toward the alley where she had come from and as we approached, I saw her companion coming from the other direction holding a plastic shopping bag. He opened it up and I saw seven boxes of Twinkies and a six-pack of Dr. Pepper inside. Now they were both beaming with happiness. As this unusual couple returned to their ship I begged them to tell me who they were, what was so important about Twinkies, and if I could have one or two.

They patiently explained that they were from the far distant future of Earth and that each Twinkie was capable of producing a thousand-year supply of antimatter for their giant matter-antimatter reactor. The mega-power plant had been built by an advanced civilization discovered living near the center of the earth, and those peace-loving people had subsequently been conquered and enslaved.

Anyway, they were about to use up their last Twinkie and had returned to our time to get more. I was quite surprised and a bit skeptical, to say the least. (I'm going to have to buy a box and double-check the ingredients.) I inquired about the Dr. Pepper and they explained that they just like to drink Dr. Pepper, and not the diet stuff.

She smiled at me one last time, put the disc into the panel, and they entered the time machine to terminate their visit. I thought that was pretty cool and attempted to follow, but the force field knocked me out.

The next thing I remember was a steady tugging at my feet. When I opened my eyes, the ship was gone and there was a homeless guy running away with my shoes.

FIREFLY

After hatching and wandering about for days, Pierre the firefly finally found a place that was perfect for finding a Mrs. Firefly. The grass was sweet and long and stretched for as far as his eyes could see. The future seemed bright, but things are not always as they appear.

One peaceful afternoon, as he was sunning himself in preparation for the dusk's activities, a firefly wearing a powdered wig flew over and struck up a conversation.

"You are new here," declared the fashionable firefly with a French accent, "so allow me to introduce myself. I am Dr. Guillotin. If you haven't heard, there is revolution afoot which will climax tomorrow at noon, and I want to know if you will join us."

Dr. Guillotin further explained that Louis, the local king of the fireflies, was a tyrant and "not the brightest bulb." Plans had been hatched to depose him and replace the monarchy with a representational form of government. Pierre was intrigued and agreed to be on their side, and Dr. Guillotin headed off to recruit some European Starlings.

That evening, as chance would have it, Pierre met a lovely young lady firefly named Renée. What Pierre did not know was that she belonged to the King's court and often carried covert communiques to loyalists in the outlying regions. Their love blossomed instantly and caused her to regret her royal involvement. She realized she must leave the court and fly away with Pierre to start a family, so after a flashy evening of song and dance she returned to the palace to put her affairs in order, feed her goldfish, and secretly pack her trunk.

The next day, the attack was launched and a lot of troops on both sides were killed by the starlings. All day long the battle raged. Evening fell and found the insurgents fighting with the King's Guard in the palace itself. That's when Pierre and his comrades spied Renée in her regal garb and confronted her. He felt betrayed, and she tried to impress upon him that she was leaving that life because of their love. He did not believe her and flew into the night to be alone and sulk. Renée was captured and placed in an empty beer bottle along with the royal family and their entourage.

The following day was filled with feasts and a parade, and afterward the trial of the prisoners began. Pierre felt guilty for the way he had flown off and petitioned the court on Renée's behalf. Her hearing was postponed for a day so Pierre could prepare her defense. He sat at a small wooden desk in the library and worked far into the evening. After finishing a particularly difficult but brilliant legal point, he flew outside for some fresh air.

Suddenly, he was captured and put into a coffee can by two boys, Scooter and Biff, who were outside playing after dark without mother's permission. They were thoughtful enough to poke holes in the lid, and later on he had to share the can with an annoyingly happy-go-lucky beetle named Brent.

And there poor Pierre remained, desperately climbing up and down the twigs amidst the grass clippings, frustrated and heartbroken, until he expired. Renée never learned why he didn't return, but her love did not falter for an instant. She was found guilty of being a spy and was sentenced to death.

Their love was a rare and wondrous thing and it never died. It did, however, smell pretty bad after a few days.

DOUGHNUT

Mr. Latmus (age 49, married) didn't notice that the lights had changed as he endeavored to cross the busy street while listening to the Beatles "A Day in the Life" on his iPhone, and he got honked at by some clown in a Jeep.

Mr. Latmus was coming from the office to get a quick snack and coffee at the corner store during break time, and again he played the scene of their morning meeting in his head. All employees in the loan processing department of Moon Mortgage had just been given their two-week dismissal notice. He had been at that company for over three years and now he was being discarded like an old boot. No one was happy, but they had heard the rumors so they were not totally surprised.

Mr. Latmus ordered a chocolate glazed doughnut and black coffee, paid, and returned to his cubicle on the third floor. Upon opening the bag he spied a solitary ant munching cheerfully on the doughnut.

"Oh crap," he mumbled to himself. He flicked the ant into his metal wastebasket and after a little reflection, put the doughnut back in the bag and brought it as a gift to his supervisor who was busy on the phone, and returned to his desk. The supervisor, Mr. Endymion, looked in the bag when he had the chance, noted it with disdain because he was dieting, and took the bag to *his* manager, Selene, at their afternoon meeting in the conference room. She graciously accepted the gift.

After the meeting, Selene made sure she was the last one out of the room. She took the bag containing the doughnut and quietly dropped it into the first wastebasket she passed, which happened to be at Mr. Latmus' desk.

When he returned from the washroom, he noticed the bag and glanced inside. There was that doughnut again! After a bit of consternation he believed it best to leave it there and say nothing, assuming that his boss was sending him some sort of rude message.

Meanwhile, the ant had been running in endless circles searching the basket for a way of escape, but found nothing except sheets of crumpled paper and a bit of dried-up chewing gum. He was unable to scale the wall and wished he knew how to build a ladder or something useful. Why hadn't he paid more attention in school? Soon his frustration turned to despair, and the ant's brain went inexorably down the windowless corridor of insanity.

Consequently, you can imagine his delight when the bag and doughnut came hurtling back to him after three and a half hours. He scrambled onto the pastry with joy in his heart, clung to it and wept, and gorged himself on the treat. He was so happy that he barely noticed later when he and his surroundings were poured into another basket. The next thing he knew, he was being tossed, with his doughnut, into the dumpster outside.

Feeling satisfied and at peace with the world, he climbed out through a rusty hole at the bottom of the container, strolled back to his intricate network of tunnels, and returned to the forest whistling a happy tune. Life can be really good sometimes.

Mr. Latmus, after being laid off, ended up flipping burgers and asking, "Do you want fries with that shake?" for the next two years. Mr. Endymion and Selene had a brief, unsatisfying relationship; she liked him best when he was sleeping. They kept their jobs another year until the next round of layoffs.

The ant was motivated to go on to night school where he studied really hard and became a carpenter...ant.

Unfortunately, a year later he secretly murdered his entire family with a torque wrench.

I told you he was going insane, but did anyone listen to me? Noooo....

THE GLOOMY-BIRD

It was a day as hot as the flaming forge of Vulcan in the sleepy little village when, circling high overhead, came...the Gloomy-Bird! The locals knew something terrible was about to occur, as it had one hundred years ago when this monstrous creature last appeared out of the wilderness. Their folklore was filled with tales of the horrific black vulture of doom, with its 32 foot wingspan, that could snatch up and carry off full-grown men as if they were cheap ragdolls. Word spread like wildfire.

Peering out the window of their cottage, young Scooter and Biff wondered aloud if they would be affected by this new turn of events. They watched the gigantic bird making wide leisurely circles as it floated on the shimmering blue sky, but Mother shooed them from the window.

She cried out, "Now dontcha be bringin' dat bad luck onta dis house, I'm-a tellin' youse kids. You getcha back ta yer room an' dontcha let dat Gloomy-Bird sees ya, I tells ya dat!" Scooter and Biff ran to their room and shut the door.

"Why do people here have to talk with that quaint, rustic accent?" Scooter asked rhetorically. "Mother is murdering the language, just like everyone else in this sleepy little village. I love her, but she is a bumpkin. Incidentally, did you know the word 'bumpkin' likely comes from the Middle Dutch word 'boomekijn' meaning 'small barrel'?"

"Yes, you are indeed correct," replied Biff, using perfect articulation. "Besides, I am not afraid of the Gloomy-Bird and I certainly do not believe in old wives' tales." They were both ready for a bit of excitement. In the meantime, Mother had lit the stone fireplace and was nailing closed all the shutters and doors while muttering under her breath.

In town, the bravest men gathered weapons as the police chief organized the militia and the mayor set up a command post on the top floor of the town hall. From there, the council could see the entire countryside and give orders if and when they agreed on what to do. One gentleman wanted to put up a big sign that read "Nobody Home" and have everyone hide in their basements, but he had to argue with another who insisted on putting up a big sign that read "Go Away," who then leaned out of the Tudor-style window and brazenly flipped the bird a bird of his own.

All afternoon the Gloomy-Bird watched the village, slowly drifting lower and lower. Fear consumed the land as people hunkered down in their houses. Some got drunk and partied like there was no tomorrow while others wept openly. Woodland creatures cowered in their burrows and birds quailed under their nests. Even the village idiot was scared; he ran through the narrow cobblestone streets with a potato tied to his belt crying "Fowl" until someone pushed him into a root cellar.

Meanwhile, Scooter and Biff, totally disregarding Mother's instructions, forced open their window and ran to a clearing in a nearby field to get a better view of the big bird. Suddenly, with a bloodcurdling screech, the Gloomy-Bird swooped down, clutched the boys in its gigantic talons, and flew upward, beating its huge black wings against the hot summer air.

"Isn't this exciting?" shouted Scooter to his brother.

"It certainly is!" yelled Biff as the Gloomy-Bird soared away to disappear for another hundred years.

The elders of the village observed all this from their perch above the town hall.

"Oh well," said the mayor to the gathered council, "…never did like dem smart-alecky kids, I tells ya dat."

STRAY BULLETS
(A STRANGE INTERLUDE)

The new couple moved in uneventfully that spring morning next to the sheriff's house. Nobody appeared to notice them. Folks keep to themselves pretty much around here, if you get what I mean. Do you, stranger?

Nina, the lady of the house, grew and sold flowers in the front yard and her mate, Sam, had six white horses he kept around in back. Also, and this is a bit unusual, they had a calico cat named Bobby that could talk in a whisper, only at midnight, for fifteen minutes. After that, it became a little hoarse and stopped. The best explanation for it is that the cat was born in a place and time where the nine dimensions folded onto each other for a moment, then snapped back to their rightful places. (Come to think of it, that would explain a lot of things in this book.)

It was rumored that the couple came from Lithuania and used to work at a board game factory. Sam now worked for a funeral parlor and part-time as a writer, but secretly he was scamming off of his cat, which they had renamed Boris. He had been pawning off stories about seafood, napping, and love triangles as his own, but no one would publish him anymore and the checks came to a halt.

"Past his prime," the publishers all agreed. His stories had become as predictable as old Roy Lopez coming to deliver the mail every day. Nina was nice but rather plain, and they got along well together...until the issue of paying taxes came up. She thought her Sam was a little crazy when it came to avoiding taxes.

You can imagine the dismay when one morning Sam could not find his cat. A stray bullet had shattered the bathroom window the night before and the feline had darted out of their comfy castle, thankful for its freedom, and changed its name back to Bobby.

Weeks later, due to stress and garden neglect, the wife had trouble with the bishop's weed encroaching on her peonies. The horses were complaining about the rain and wishing they had a king-sized stable to live in, but Sammy wouldn't hear of it. The couple wondered if having a child would make life better, since the cat was gone.

Young Staunton was eight years old when the couple adopted him, and he was promptly renamed Boris. He did not have much talent for stories, but it didn't matter; life returned to normal. The man was writing again, this time about monsters, candy, and running away from home, and the flowers were flourishing once more.

Black Knight Publishing took a long shot and printed one of his collections of prose on the aforementioned subjects. The book was a flop, and the publisher felt he had been rooked. Sam accepted the failure *en passant* and strategically inflated his tax loss.

Late one evening a year later, a stray bullet hit the front doorknob and Boris took the gambit, darting out and heading straight for the railroad tracks. Time to change his name back and find a normal family.

After that, due to stress and neglect, Nina had problems with her Eglantine roses and the Queen Anne's lace she was growing. They developed those tiny, yellow, crawly bugs; what do you call those? She struggled to get rid of them but was constantly met with a stalemate. The horses still complained about the rain and how they were only exercised when there was a funeral carriage to pull.

The couple considered taking lessons to learn to play checkers; that's a popular thing to do around here – that and minding your own business...stranger.

A month later, Sam was writing once more, this time about eating hay, rearing up, and getting in out of the rain.

Some people have no originality.

MY GREATEST FEAR

Everyone has things they are afraid of, real and imaginary. I want to share mine with you in the hope that by naming it, I'll free myself of this paralyzing fear and find peace.

I keep my drapes closed and avoid going outside as much as possible because I am filled with dread that one day while I'm out gazing at the horizon, an enormous head will pop up, a head occupying about half the sky. Something like that would destroy all my beliefs concerning life and reality; it would be like a scene out of *The Twilight Zone* (an old science-fiction TV program). I have no inkling of what the head would do or say, but the mere fact of its existence would be enough to scare the living crap out of me. Not sure why, but I have had this phobia ever since I was young and my parents took me to a Thanksgiving Day parade.

There is nowhere to run, no way to escape this gigantic face looking at our puny world. And each person that became aware of it would know that the head was looking at them personally, delving into their deepest thoughts and secrets. I suppose it would matter to some if the head was male or female, or had a big white beard or red horns or pink ribbons in its hair, but those are only cultural descriptors. I picture it as a father-figure with a stern expression, looking us over in a curious yet detached kind of way.

Or, what if this massive head appeared and I was the only one who could see it? That would really be messed up because if I tried to warn others, the authorities would point at me and declare, "This fellow, right here, is mentally unbalanced," and confine me in an asylum for the terminally imaginative so I could experience a little electroconvulsive therapy. That could be weird.

Now you might say I've sat in the sun too long or read

too many comic books as a kid, but that's not the point. This is something I feel could actually happen. There are not enough aluminum foil hats in the world to protect me, and vodka therapy has been useless so far.

And what if the giant head simply stayed there, not doing or saying anything, but watching and waiting? I'd be as nervous as a long-tailed cat in a garage full of laser activated, high-speed, electric rocking chairs! It has to be there for a purpose. Maybe I can reason with it and find out.

"Hello, Head? Do you hear me? Head?" No, it won't answer from wherever it's hiding right now.

Perhaps it will be a sign for me, like I'm destined to change the world or something. I could tell people my opinions and if they disagreed, I'd announce, "Oh yeah? Well, the Colossal Head in the sky says I'm right and you're wrong, so there!"

That should win more than a few arguments.

Possibly if I fired weapons at it, the head would go back where it came from. A gun would not be enough; I'd need a surface-to-air missile, or bigger. Perhaps a giant laser beam would scare it away, or one of those new rail guns that I could probably purchase from certain local teenagers.

Oh, who am I kidding? It won't leave no matter what I do. I know I said that naming my fear would help me, but I think I've made it worse. Not only that, but I'll bet that I have now infected you, the reader, with this same anxiety; waiting for the hour when that terrible head pops up over the horizon and finds us with its burning gaze.

Amazing Ants
(A One-Act Tragedy)

Deep in the forest there lived a huge colony of ants. It was a typical group: queen, drones, carpenters, harvesters, janitors, soldiers, and a few crazy ants like any well-ordered society. One of the crazy carpenter ants was named Duncan, and he loved to go exploring through the forest, dunes, and nearby city. And he always found his way home!

Duncan was also quite the engineer after he finished night school, having invented some ingenious hand-tools. After a while, all the ants knew of his navigational prowess and it was decreed that he should be forced to help compose and illustrate an all-inclusive map for Ant-Queen Atreides. Of course, he had hard feelings about that imposition and wished for a way to get even.

Using his excellent memory, Duncan described the many miles of tunnels to the scribes and the cartographer. This took, all told, roughly nine months. When it was completed, the Queen declared a feast day and everyone got to see the marvelous map and enjoy a big, delicious slice of apple sponge-cake á la Annie. Insects from all across the forest celebrated this remarkable feat, declaring that they were now entering into their "post-modern" era.

Subsequently, their technology advanced even further and radios and miniature ant cell-phones were invented. Communications and logistics improved greatly, which tended to promote more free time. A group of ants formed a glee club and did a performance of "Ant Misbehavin'." Another one became a philosopher who taught that the colony couldn't know anything for certain; his name was Immanuel K. Ant. As you might imagine, their culture that had once been rigid and responsible soon became loose and laid-back...then came the winter.

Power outages occurred because unconcerned worker

ants were calling in sick when they weren't, and water became scarce as not enough fire ants were willing to go out and collect snow. Children ants were being disrespectful to the adults. Soon the Queen had enough of it all, so she gathered all the ants to make a speech.

She took the microphone, cleared her throat, and announced, "We have become amazing ants. I believe we've outgrown this network of tunnels and should evolve to a higher level of existence. If we wish hard enough and believe, then it will happen. We deserve this!" A drastic change would reorder their odd behavior, she supposed, and the ants would get serious again. Hopefully their very DNA would mutate without making them all sterile and they'd become a new, superior species. The ants all nodded their approval and the concept took a firm hold in their collective consciousness.

"We resolve to evolve!" the ants chanted together, and soon their voices filled the forest. Since they had a catchy slogan, they packed their suitcases and, examining the map, headed for an unknown and distant place that surely held great promise. Duncan had labeled one of the remote tunnel destinations as "Star's End" and drew a happy face next to it. A bright Golden Path awaited them all. The enormous swarm of ants began the journey, certain that life was about to become better. No one bothered to consult Duncan and he stayed behind.

The Queen, who was leading them, often had to stop and repeat to herself, "I must not fear. Fear is the mind-killer." After a long and dreary journey, the herd arrived at their paradise and, one by one, walked unknowingly out of the dark and into the mouths of the hungry anteaters at the City Zoo. Unfortunately for Duncan, Queen Atreides uttered a powerful curse at him with her final breath.

They had all gone to their doom except the lonely carpenter ant who, several weeks later, died screaming from Rectal Chronic Pervasive Disorder.

CAT RADIO

The cat woke up and stretched slowly while lying in the warm sunshine outside the stately mansion where he lived, then yawned and licked a paw. The feline was a typical short-hair calico breed, perhaps four years old, but cats are not always as they seem. The animal suddenly got an idea, jumped up, and rushed inside at full speed. He found his owner and jumped onto his lap meowing that he wanted to write and star in a radio drama. Yes, it was the magical cat named Bobby who had mutated past his hoarseness and could speak freely now.

Harvey, the homeowner, was rich because the cat dreamt up stories that Harvey transcribed, edited, and published and some of the books had become popular. Most of the stories were about seafood, napping, and unusual love triangles, but they were entertaining if you were fond of cats (all except his science book *A Brief History of Cats*, which was an unmitigated catastrophe).

So they talked it over, and it was agreed that Bobby would try his paw at writing for radio. Harv and the cat wrote and rewrote the manuscript until they had what they hoped was a masterpiece entitled *Kitty on a Hot Tin Roof*. At its completion, Harvey boasted, "Bobby, I am more creative as a writer than you are."

"Wouldn't it be funny if that was true," replied Bobby with a wink of his eye.

The next week, an open casting call was placed in the local newspapers and online. Their production company was fortunate enough to recruit the illustrious Chicago Sympathy Orchestra, conducted by Phil Harmonic, to play the background music. The theme song was adapted from an old tune called "Kitty" by a cat named Stevens.

The paunchy, balding sheriff of the town learned of the tryouts so he went to audition at the mansion, mainly because he wanted a look-see inside that impressive brick residence. He waited patiently in line behind all the Hollywood stars and a few high school kids. (One of the kids kept howling like a wolf and had to be escorted out, the big idiot.)

After two hours of waiting and being snubbed by "them richy-rich folks," the sheriff got his chance. Going to the microphone with a script and a smirk on his face, he meowed like a sick cat, "Meeowrr-rrrow" and grinned like a fool, much to the annoyance of Bobby, who held his paws over his ears after hearing the unearthly cry of the sheriff. The sheriff had no clue what the play was about and since he was there on false pretenses, he had a sudden craving to bluff his way out by being annoying and showing he was just as good as them city slickers.

Becoming completely fed up with his performance, the cat jumped down from his upholstered director's chair, circled around behind, and catapulted himself onto the sheriff's head with his claws out. The sheriff pulled his gun in surprise and confusion and a stray bullet hit the electrician in the arm. The electrician fell and pulled down enough plugs and wires to send electricity through a dozen microphones, zapping a lot of the actors and stagehands. Everybody started cursing and running around in such confusion that the cat got scared and ran under a table. There he found the stunt-mouse, which he chased out of the building and around the grounds for twenty minutes. Then Bobby took a nap.

During the confusion, Harvey went and hid behind the icebox while the associate producer kept apologizing to everyone, and the sheriff slithered back to town without a word. The Hollywood people flew home angry and insulted and the entire event was cancelled.

The next day, the cat's staff members were still wondering what had actually happened, and the magical tabby totally lost interest in radio drama.

After all, there was the *Theatre* to think of!

WRITER'S BLOCK

I seem to have gotten a case of writer's block. I sit at the computer and stare at the screen but can't think of anything to write. I can't even think of other people's stories to change slightly and pretend they're mine, or take something I wrote long ago and improve it. I can't produce evidence at this time, but I believe local llamas are selectively stealing my thoughts. Your first question might be, why llamas? Why not idea-stealing giraffes or eagles? Well, why *not* llamas? In my humble opinion, that blank expression is merely a cunning disguise to mask the evil that lurks within. There's a pair of them, one male and one female, which are hacking into my brain.

I lock all the doors and windows and go to my desk to try to write something amusing, and my notion starts bubbling up like one of those little mud geysers at Yellowstone Park. The llamas sense this and their ears suddenly perk up as I'm about to have my revelation. Then -blap- there's nothing left but stinky gas and my idea is gone.

And what are they doing with my thoughts? I believe they are funneling them to a Chinese humorist whom I'll call Mr. X. If I could read any of his stories I'd probably crack up laughing, if I could read and understand Chinese. But since I can't prove it, I can't get any money from him. If I went to the police or to court to sue, I'd likely be sent to the asylum for the terminally imaginative and medicated into a stupor.

What I need to do is find a pair of pandas in China to take my ideas away from Mr. X and return them to me. They would have to be re-translated into English on the computer and may sound out of order at first, but I think I could make them humorous again if I worked really hard. Or, better yet, I could look for bilingual pandas! I wonder if there's a brochure for that somewhere I could send for.

The nearest llamas I know of are in the zoo, but it's likely that this pair is hiding at a nearby farm. I sent two of my balloon friends to search for them, but the llamas probably sent starlings to intercept the balloons so they couldn't return (Goodbye Fred and Carrie). But even if I found these llamas, what could I do?

Maybe there are aluminum bicycle helmets with the ears cut out and chin straps that I could force onto their evil heads. I thought I had a way to locate them just now, but those smelly, four-legged fiends have stolen that thought from me as well, so now they've been tipped off and might be moving to a different farm. Dang it!

Since I've lost my creativity, I'll digress a bit. The term Writer's Block first appeared in 1947 from the research of Edmund Bergler M.D. (1899–1962) He theorized that it was a neurotic inhibition of productivity in creative writers. Edmund was a Freudian and stated that most people were addicted to unresolved negative emotions, which is part of their psychic masochism. He spent twenty years on his theories and they were not well received for some reason. I have no inclination to look that deeply into my writer's block because I *know* there are llamas to blame!

I think if I ever do catch up to those wicked quadrupeds, I'll simply have them shot dead and shrunk down and stuffed, and I'll put them in a display case in my basement. My girlfriend can sew cute outfits for them to wear instead of dressing up the poor cat. My writer's block will disappear and I'll be funny again.

Then I'll invite everyone over to see the dolly llamas.

Laugh, Clown!

Once there was a traveling circus that visited small towns and villages and had pretty good success. With them was a troupe of five clowns who had developed some very amusing skits that both children and adults really enjoyed. The clowns felt blessed in finding their true calling in life and their relationship to each other was good on the surface, but clowns are not always as they seem.

Bleepy, the shortest of the clowns, had a hidden passion that none of the others knew about. He loved bunny rabbits and, deep inside, he longed to be one. Bleepy understood that he could not tell anyone because he would face ridicule and rejection, so he kept his bunny costume well-hidden and only put it on when he was alone and sure he had plenty of time to enjoy it.

One day, Plooky the clown came back unexpectedly early from town in the Jeep and spied Bleepy through the trailer window dressed in his outfit, hopping about playfully and nibbling on carrots. Plooky quietly departed and waited for the rest of the clowns to arrive, by which time Bleepy was back to his regular self.

"So, Bleepy," said Plooky when they were all together, "What have *you* been doing today?" His tone of voice carried implications.

"Not much," the nervous clown answered softly. Then there passed a long silence as Bleepy kept his eyes on the floor while Plooky applied lotion to his spider-bite rash.

Days later, during their weekly meeting, it was Plooky who brought up the idea of a new routine wherein one of them might dress up like a rabbit and cavort about the ring. The clowns discussed the concept and they agreed upon the logical choice – they'd chase the rabbit with big nets. Bleepy volunteered to be the rabbit but not too quickly so that no one would suspect him of any ulterior motive, but deep inside he was thrilled. He was thankful that, after more discussion, it would replace the skit where they chased him with Tasers.

Bleepy came in the next day and pretended he had just bought his costume, but Plooky knew otherwise and quietly plotted his revenge. All this is because Bleepy had once embarrassed him in front of a cute waitress during a breakfast conversation at the Waffle House. Bleepy had pointed out the clown's ignorance of classic movie trivia when Plooky couldn't remember Dorothy's last name from *The Wizard of Oz*, and then laughed at him. (Have you any idea how hard it is to get a date with a waitress when you inform her that you are a traveling, professional clown?) Time went by and they practiced their new skit constantly at Bleepy's insistence.

That fateful evening, the circus began as usual with the trapeze artists followed by the lion tamer and a rude, pint-sized monkey comedian. After that, Bleepy, fully dressed in his rabbit costume, came hopping joyfully into the center ring. Ten seconds later, Plooky ran in carrying a giant carrot and then the last three clowns entered swinging huge butterfly nets. The whole audience was laughing as he chased the carrot this way and that while avoiding the nets. Around and around they went until they all converged in the middle of the ring, and Bleepy was captured as he caught the carrot. The audience broke into applause, and the clowns took their bow.

After the noise had subsided, Plooky snuck up behind Bleep, yanked off his fake ears, and shoved him forward while shouting for the multitude to hear, "Hey everybody, he secretly dresses like this in private." Plooky turned to Bleepy and yelled, "*Now* laugh, clown!" and strode away. The crowd stared at the little clown silently, judging him. Bleepy smiled bravely but was utterly humiliated, and a part of him died that day.

Two weeks later, in another town, the news media reported that a clown named Plooky was hit by a Jeep driven by a giant, unknown rabbit.

WELCOME WAGON

A pleasant smile settled on old Doris's expression as she approached the door of the new residents in the college-town apartment building where she lived, and reaching it, she hesitated.

Doris was about five foot four and rather thin, wearing her prim and proper pastel pink dress with matching pillbox hat, white gloves and her gray hair in a bun, all designed to make a wholesome impression. She considered herself the official self-appointed Welcome Wagon committee. Beside her purse she carried a wicker basket containing cheese and crackers, a small jar of olives, a potted fern, a little ceramic mouse which symbolized poverty, several old coupon books, and a slightly inaccurate hand-drawn map of the town. Knowing what to bring to new residents was important to her.

In contrast, when she had moved in, all she got was ignored during the day and loud music up to 2:30 at night. Rap music frightened her. One apartment occasionally cranked up the march from *The Love for Three Oranges* by the classical composer Prokofiev, which was disturbing and most unexpected. Everyone continued to ignore her except some of the women who said hello from time to time in the hallway when they couldn't avoid it.

Doris took a deep breath and raised her gloved hand to knock, and froze as her mind flashed back to the week she had moved in. An unknown person had written the word "Spinster" in ink in tiny letters on her door. That hurt! Recently, someone had spilled beer on her welcome doormat and her newspaper went missing. She fancied herself like a mother to these students, and this is how they repaid her kindness? What ever happened to respecting your elders and just being nice?

She stood there, sad and bewildered, with unresolved negative emotions welling up inside. Then something in her snapped. The heck with them all! She dug around in her bag until she found her magic marker then wrote DORKS on their door in big black letters and returned to her apartment to feel sorry for herself.

The next day, the old landlord, Gus, visited her for tea at two in the afternoon and asked suspiciously if she had seen the new tenants yet. She replied that she was planning to go today with her happy-basket of cheer and welcome them. He gave her a funny look, wondered if she was interested in him, and hoped she wasn't going to pull any psychological dependency games. She imagined he was interested in her and had all kinds of excuses ready to discourage his reckless advances. They were friends, nevertheless, for Doris had given him a fern. Actually, she had bought a lot of fern plants wholesale and would give them as gifts to people, churches, and businesses all over town for what she termed "beautification."

After tea, Doris again carried her happy-basket to the new people's door, read her handiwork, and began to laugh. Dorks! Harder and harder she laughed until she dropped the basket and slumped to the carpeted floor in hysterics. The occupants heard this and opened their door to see what the commotion was.

Seeing the figure on the floor, one whispered to the other, "This is the old gal they warned us about." Listening to her infectious laughter made them feel happy yet kind of embarrassed, and soon they were laughing along with her, which made Doris laugh even harder. After several minutes she regained a bit of composure, mostly due to oxygen deprivation and fatigue. The pair helped Doris to her feet whereupon she brushed herself off and handed them their basket.

"Welcome to the building, Dorks," she said with a smirk, and walked away.

Another successful Welcome Wagon visit.

WERE-PIGS

Everyone has heard of were-wolves, but have you ever heard of were-pigs? I hadn't until a critical incident transpired in my life. Please allow me to explain.

It was a full moon that evening I first visited one of those all-you-can-eat restaurants. I was walking to my seat between rows of tables when I spotted a five-dollar bill on the floor. So, being a nice guy, I picked it up and handed it to the guy sitting there. As soon as it was within his reach, he rapidly jerked his head and bit me on the arm. It broke the skin a bit but I didn't realize I was cut at the time, and I moved on after giving him a dirty look and wanting to challenge him to a death-duel, but I kept my mouth shut. He continued his eating frenzy and totally ignored me. Incidentally, the best part of those restaurants is that you can have all the dessert you want. (Try it sometime, they won't stop you.)

The next day, I noticed the spot was red and swollen, so I put some salve on it before driving to work. But on the way there I abruptly became aware that I was chewing on my hat. I was overcome with an appetite like I have never known in my life. Pulling into the nearest fast-food joint, I ordered a double cheeseburger and fries and ate faster than I ever have, but it was not enough. I returned to the counter and ordered seven more burgers, ten fries, and three apple pies, and after eating all that I was *still* famished! It was weird because I had never felt such a hunger before in my life and I wondered, "Is this what starvation feels like?"

I called in sick to work and drove to the grocery store where I nearly maxed out my checking account. I drove away with bulging bags of groceries and once home, I started cooking and eating: pizzas, chips, gallons of soft drinks, hot-dogs and hamburgers, peanut butter and jelly sandwiches, rice, raw fruits and vegetables, boxes of cereal, gallons of milk, kitty litter, pork chops with apple sauce, candy and ice cream, cookies, bags of flour, eggs, truffles with caviar, olives, buffalo wings, soup, spaghetti, giant burritos, tacos, steaks, chickens, bacon, and a bunch of stuff with bacon already in it and after four hours, I felt normal again.

But I realized it would soon be dinnertime, and then what would I do? I could not afford to go shopping until next payday. At that point I conveniently remembered the all-you-can-eat restaurant. I drove back in the evening and, sure enough, that guy was at the same table so I sat opposite him for a confrontation. He was so busy eating that he didn't notice me until I grabbed a chicken wing from his plate, which made him look up and growl. I growled right back as I stuffed it in my mouth.

"What in the world did you do to me?" I yelled. He was going to keep ignoring me so I started reaching for another chicken wing. This made him stop eating, and he grudgingly explained that during the full moon almost everyone there was a were-pig, having been bitten by another were-pig at some point in time, and it made sense. I got up, took a plate, and after filling it to overflowing I returned to his table where we both ate silently for hours, pausing only for refills.

This restaurant has become my new home several days per month. The customers are like family to me in that we eat and eat and pretty much ignore each other. My only complaint is the table of guys all wearing plaid golf pants; they seem angry at me for some reason.

So, if you decide to visit when the moon is full and bright, and are not one of us, keep your arms close to your sides as you walk through or you might become a were-pig yourself.

HAPPINESS

Ricardo (not his real name) was walking around the building where he worked during lunch-hour for exercise, wondering why he felt lower than a snake's belly in a wheel rut. There was no obvious reason for it. He should have been happy. After all, he had a decent temp job, was in a pretty good relationship, and had food and shelter. Plus, the old car ran well most of the time despite its rusting apart and being a money-pit.

There were times when he felt very happy, peak moments now and then, such as being told he was doing a good job by his supervisor, observing his girlfriend while listening to "Stardust" by Louis Armstrong, or watching a humorous movie. Ricardo wished those feelings would last longer. He wondered if others felt the same way but didn't want to raise the subject for fear that his friends would think he was being a big baby. He was expected to act happy no matter what he was feeling deep inside. Depression was not something his family talked about.

After his exercise, he went back in and lost himself in work, forgetting his melancholy for a while. Driving home afterwards, he thought about ways to be happier but couldn't come up with anything. He knew individuals who seemed to be happy all the time and wondered if their brains were somehow different than his.

That night he went up on the roof to ponder what he wanted in life, where he was going, and if it was possible to truly understand and appreciate life without taking into account a higher power or deity. After staring at the moon for an hour, Ricardo got his great revelation. He would eat the brains of his happiest friends and see if that didn't cheer him up from the inside.

The first brain he ate didn't seem to do much. In fact, he felt somewhat guilty about it; perhaps it was slightly undercooked. The second brain helped a bit more. He laughed maniacally and felt great, but after two weeks it wore thin. Now the third brain, that one did the trick.

He was smiling constantly and laughing at every little thing. This time the joy and elation didn't fade. People wondered at the change in him, but he dared not reveal his secret. Life was good, but after seven months the effect started waning and he felt the urge for another happy-brain meal. Since all his cheeriest friends were gone, he had to find new ones to replace them with, and quick.

Ricardo began frequenting various comedy clubs and soon met many more happy people who provided a fresh supply of gray matter to meet his unusual need. Ricardo was so blissful all the time now that one club hired him to do a stand-up routine, and he was finally able to afford a new car and went out and bought a used Prion.

Ricardo made jokes about the unemployed, obscure medical conditions, and did a bizarre skit with a sock puppet but the story I liked telling best became the one about me eating brains to stay happy. Wait a minute...I think I've said too much here. Ummmmm.

Please forget you read that part, I just made it up. Seriously. Nobody would do something as crazy as harvesting brains, would they? Of course not, don't be absurd!

By the way, how happy are you?

Subliminal message: You are very happy.

A Little Concerned

Once there were three friendly alligators that lived in a remote corner of the swamp in the Mystee forest. They loved to frolic in the water, sun themselves, and, for sport, they played soccer against the beavers and woodchucks. And the alligators always won. There was lots of tasty carrion to eat and nothing really bad had ever happened to them. Yes, existence was agreeable, but circumstances can alter without notice.

Late one afternoon while relaxing in the shallow water after a nice meal, old Butch, their leader, began to cough. At first it was routine since he already had a bad cough from years of hanging out with the hookah-smoking caterpillars, but after twenty minutes his friends had something to say.

"Hey, Butch," Larry called, "what are you doing coughing so much? Food go down the wrong pipe?" Butch didn't answer but waved his paw and pointed to his throat.

Then Mary chimed in, "Hey Butch, what do you want us to do, call out the National Guard?" and she grinned at him. They both watched as Butch continued to cough and it didn't seem to be getting better. Now Mary and Larry became a little concerned.

They tried a home remedy that alligators often use and gave him a plug of swamp grass to chew. That didn't work, although it did help his breath considerably. Next they gave him a glass of fish oil mixed with a shot of rum to drink. Again, this caused no change whatsoever in his cough but did make him burp in between.

Talk spread among the critters of the swamp that something was seriously wrong with Butch. While not a violent cough, it persisted into the evening and kept everyone awake. The beavers and woodchucks hoped he was dying and planned a party because they thought he cheated at soccer by playing too rough. A woodchuck sub-committee even budgeted to buy fireworks for the celebration although it would raise their taxes, and some were a little concerned.

Mary and Larry called for the local doctor and Timmy wanted to start with a spinal tap, but Butch smacked him away with his long, powerful tail. Around midnight it became clear that drastic measures were called for, so they consulted the Big Book of Alligator Folklore and Remedies and found the answer on page 131.

Mary and Larry took their coughing friend and laid him on a big flat rock in the light of the full moon. They wound up his tail and tucked it under him, then propped his mouth open with a stick and sprinkled water on his head. Mary and Larry began their guttural incantation while trying to come up with words that rhyme with alligator.

Following a bit of rhythmic chanting, they jumped as high as they could (which isn't much if you think about it) and both landed on his back right above his belly – an alligator Heimlich maneuver. Instantly, a large catfish popped out of Butch's throat and swam away gleefully.

"Gee," observed Mary, "looks like the catfish had his tongue." Everyone laughed, and Butch agreed not to wolf down his food anymore.

Two days later, trappers caught Butch and he was never seen in the swamp again.

Again, Mary and Larry were a little concerned.

NOTHING YET

There was no outstanding characteristic in the way Ezra Tuttle appeared or behaved that would lead you to believe he was an extraterrestrial from the planet Vormfordooz. That is to say, he was as ordinary and peculiar as the rest of us. His friends called him E.T. for short. He *was* rather short, being only five foot four, but he came from the third tallest race in the galaxy. Earthlings were taller on average, but some lovable, long-tailed blue aliens in a distant star system were the tallest of all.

His parents had dropped him off a few weeks ago for his autumn vacation. He enjoyed the fall weather and colors because his native planet was all plain gray granite and never got cooler than 451 degrees F. (incidentally, Vormfordooz was famous for its blue yogurt). However, E.T. was waiting for something really big to happen on Earth so that he could step in, reveal he was from another world, and take charge and impress people.

He watched the news every day and kept up to date with events on the Internet, but whenever he had an idea of what he could contribute, he told himself that it was too late, too far away, or his good-intentioned thoughts seemed pointless upon sober reflection. So, he stayed in his college-town apartment building, getting to know the locals and trying to learn how to socialize with humans.

To that end he liked to go to parties and sit on the couch at night pretending he was stoned or asleep while listening to their conversations. Sometimes he thought, "I just want someone to hear what I have to say. And maybe if I talk long enough, it'll make sense."

Regrettably, he had picked friends who mainly liked to get high and while he didn't learn much, they did help him feel more accepted, for which he was grateful. He had a girlfriend named Peggy but there was no romance. She was always asking Ezra for money, and he suspected people talked about how odd he was behind his back. There was also an elderly woman in the building whom he avoided. She kept offering him a fern plant which he refused, reason being he had accidentally spilled a glass of beer on her doormat and felt guilty for trying to clean it up with her newspaper. Ezra briefly joined an elite hacker group but was kicked out because all he did was go into corporate websites and capriciously post links to a book written by a turtle. Then he got addicted to various, time-consuming Internet games.

One night, as he was walking up the leaf-covered stairs, Ezra unwittingly stepped on a miniature spaceship, crushing it and the flea-sized royal family inside. Word spread quickly around the galaxy and suddenly seven worlds were at war with each other. Just as quickly, ambassadors were sent to all planets involved and last minute negotiations began. A tiny fleet of battle cruisers was dispatched to threaten E.T.'s distant world, as well as Earth. The "Force" was not with anyone; it had not been discovered yet. The only thing that came remotely close was the "Urge," which was not very helpful to anyone.

E.T. went about his daily life not realizing what had occurred, still wanting to be a part of something bigger. As he was coming back in the rain from a beer run a week later and walking along the same wet, leaf-covered porch, he inadvertently stepped on another spaceship carrying the only alien representative who could have saved the Earth. What are the odds of *that*?

The next evening, Ezra put his latest favorite song, a march by Prokofiev, on the CD player and cranked it up. Then E.T. phoned home and his doting parents inquired if anything exciting had happened to him. He rubbed his head and thought for a moment.

"Nothing yet," he replied.

Earthlings, the invasion is coming so please, watch where you step.

Rebel Frogs

Not so long ago, in the Deep South part of the swamp in the Mystee forest, there lived a trio of frogs who were the bad boys of the wetland. They controlled the place and nothing happened of which they did not first approve. The salamanders (also called mudpuppies) were all scared and careful not to make waves. The fish were frightened and stayed in school, and the turtles constantly had their soup stolen from them. No one could boss the frogs; they were the "good old boy" frogs. Other frogs stayed away from their turf since the rebel frogs would "settle their hash" if they got too close.

The only credible threat to the frogs was the cranes. A crane could fly in swiftly and snatch someone out of the water before they could remember the first stanza of "Dixie". But the cranes weren't familiar with this particular part of the swamp, and the frogs boasted that they could kick the birds' brainless butts if they had the opportunity.

One hot and humid afternoon, some of the turtles met secretly with the fish to discuss what could be done regarding those pesky polliwogs. Each idea suggested had major flaws, but they finally settled on asking the cranes to snatch up the frogs and be done with it. The dangerous part was letting the cranes know their location. Also, they were nervous about inviting outsiders to their pad and sometimes painfully shy. In fact, one of the turtles would begin to stutter if he even *thought* about unfamiliar amphibians coming to visit. A trip to the local doctor, a porcupine who claimed to know psychotherapy, failed to help him any but he did learn a lot of new cuss words to bolster his confidence with false bravado.

But back to the point, who would tell the cranes? After a heated discussion and a cheap attempt at a shell game, one of the older turtles volunteered, hoping his protective covering would offer safety. Things were arranged through a shady middleman named Norbert, and the meeting took place at the far end of the marshland during the heat of the day when the frogs were napping under the ferns.

The turtle offered the cranes not only the frogs, but also told them where to find some mudpuppies for an added incentive. The turtles had arranged to float in a line that pointed to where the frogs were so the cranes would have no difficulty picking them out. The cranes agreed to the deal then went home to contemplate their good fortune and do their silly happy dance which, if you saw it, you'd feel embarrassed for them.

A few hours later, the frogs came out to have dinner, insulting everyone in sight and mocking the turtles about their soup. The nervous turtles lined up in a row and barked, which was the signal. A moment later, the waiting cranes swooped in and each carried off a very surprised frog. Back at the bird nests, the frogs tried kicking the cranes' butts but that was an exercise in futility. Then each frog screamed and they peed themselves before being devoured.

All the swamp critters breathed a big sigh of relief and gave a cheer. Life was good again except for the bugs, which were on everyone's menu. This happy state lasted for about a week until the rebel turtles took control and became the new bad boys of the swamp.

That lasted until the cranes came back.

MUDMAN

Remember the scene from the classic holiday movie *It's A Wonderful Life* where George Bailey is ready to jump into the river because he figures he's worth more dead than alive? He later wished he had never been born. There have been times when I can identify with that, but I eventually sober up. I'm sure there are others who feel the same way, and if you do, please reconsider jumping into a dark, freezing-cold river or doing anything desperate. I have something else in mind we can try.

I have this idea of removing my clothes, getting into a large pool of mud, and covering myself from head to toe. Then I sing and dance along the side of a major highway like a drunken sailor until the police come and get me. When questioned, all I will tell them is my name is Mudman.

That's it, no other information.

They will take me to the station for further questioning, but all they will get out of me is that I am called Mudman. I'm prepared to spend a day in jail like this, and although they will probably hose me off, it won't change a thing. Of course, I'll be wearing tight underpants because I don't want a police record for indecent exposure. (Note to self: don't do this when it's cold out.)

I will appear in the police report something like "Man arrested for disorderly conduct while covered with mud." From there, the news media will pick it up, and from there, the Internet. Most likely I'll be mentioned on all the late night TV talk shows. The world will wonder who the Mudman is and what are the top ten reasons he was dancing and singing along a major highway? After that generates some publicity, I will reveal my identity, pay the fine, and hopefully be allowed to return home.

An ambitious, independent reporter will do a follow-up story and ask me why I did all that, and I'll explain that

I'm frustrated at not being able to find my ideal job. Perhaps some human resources person will then blurt out, "Hey, let's hire Mudman," because I'll now be a famous personality. I will use my new identity for good and not for evil, and I'll be a beacon of hope to others who are having trouble finding work. I will pay my bills on time, have a checking account, and even save for retirement. I will live a normal life again - as if it was ever normal to begin with.

Maybe I'll be put on a television show where I can demonstrate my wit and dancing skills, or do commercials for car dealerships. I might even start a Mudman club if I don't catch pneumonia. (Warning: I am not responsible for what happens if you jump in mud and get sick or arrested.) I am almost to the point where I will do this, but for now I feel compelled to simply write about it.

So, what do you think? Would you hire Mudman? Note: no insurance or sales jobs. Also I can't do construction or operate heavy machinery or drive an eighteen wheeler. No food service, police or security work, telemarketing, or any office job with immature co-workers or anything involving bill collections or a cash register.

I can't do anything involving landscaping, handling drugs or chemicals, or standing for eight hours like in a warehouse. I also can't do teaching, janitorial work, waste disposal, anything in a mortuary or anything to do with sharks. Also may I mention no customer service, logging, mining, raising baby dragons, fighting Orcs, protecting seven kingdoms, working in a big museum at night, supervising minions, and no more temp jobs!

I do hope to start with a three-week paid vacation and full health benefits. Working from my humble abode in my pajamas on the Internet would be a great start.

Yes indeed, Mudman is at your service.

LITTLE GREEN MEN

Tom was closing the Laundromat for the night and while locking up to leave, noticed that his frosty breath floated like ghosts in the still, February air. It had been a busy day, including mopping up a dry cleaning chemical spill, and he was tired and needed to go home and sleep.

Walking to his car under the starry sky, it occurred to him that he might have left the water running in the washroom because it had happened before and it annoyed the owner. Deciding to go in and check, he turned around just in time to catch a glimpse of a little green man a foot and a half tall with bulging black eyes dive under a bush thirty feet away. This startled him and he blinked hard several times. Tom walked over and peered under the scrubby bush. Nothing.... He walked quickly back to the door, wondering if his senses were under assault.

Taking out his keys, they accidentally dropped from his unsteady hand and as he bent to retrieve them, noticed another green man duck his head around the corner of the building next to his. He ran over, looked around warily, but didn't see anyone so he returned.

A feeling of apprehension spread through him as he entered and moved cautiously to the rear where the water indeed dribbled out. Turning off the faucet plunged the building into a deathly silence.

Tom felt he was being watched, and the hairs on the back of his neck stood up as a tingle went down his spine. Imagining all kinds of horrors of alien abduction, he knew they meant to paralyze him with ray guns and capture and probe him. Then they'd transport him to the penal colony on the planet Shargmuth in another star system where he'd be subject to their medical experiments followed by confinement in some bizarre human zoo, and they'd feed on his raw emotions for decades to come! Perhaps one day, for cheap entertainment, they'd remove his head and fill it with helium. Suddenly, he heard strange voices and his fear mushroomed.

Stepping hesitantly into the main room, he saw a tiny green man hop into one of the open dryers. Tom raced to the machine and banged the door shut. In desperation he slammed in three quarters and as it started to rotate, tiny shouts of pain reached his ears. A glance through the circular window revealed several green, contorted bodies flailing about with looks of terror on their hideous faces.

He staggered back a few paces right before the door blew open and the creatures were flung out. They wobbled and spun on the floor as if in a slow-motion nightmare. Tom was beside himself with fear and revulsion, and instinctively kicked them as hard as he could.

"You must die!" he screamed, "Die, will you?" He grabbed a laundry sack, scooped their limp bodies into it and, gripping the top tightly, frantically whipped the bag against the floor over and over in a state of panic-heightened awareness until he was exhausted.

Tom took the unopened bag to his car and considered driving to the sheriff's office. No, that would mean endless questions and possibly a charge of murder, not to mention the risk of a stray bullet. He drove them instead to the little Dispensationalist church on the outskirts of town, tied the bag to the front doorknob, and jumped back into his car. As he sped off, the steeple bell rang and he looked up at the cold, twinkling sky and wondered if aliens went to heaven when they died.

Next morning, the pastor opened a mysterious sack tied to his door and found inside the remains of three smashed-up fern plants.

The Hippie Elephant

One ordinary, warm summer afternoon a family of friendly warthogs went into the forest to forage for something to eat. They helped themselves to all kinds of apples, grapes, celery, and walnuts and frolicked playfully with one another. When the warthogs were good and tired they found a nice spot under a shady dogwood tree to take their nap. As they were resting, a dwarf elephant approached dressed in a tie-dye shirt with swinging love beads and a purple amulet on a silver chain around her neck, carrying a new alligator purse while listening to Grateful Dead music on her boom box.

"Faaaar out there," said Stella the hippie pygmy pachyderm. "What are you all doing under this my groovy tree way out here in the forest, man?"

"We're resting and minding our own business...man," replied Father nervously.

"Don't mess with me, man!" snapped Stella, "I've been to the *edge!* I've *seen* the other side, so you beat feet right now before I freak out." Stella exhaled sharply, which made everyone flee from her bad breath, then sat down and casually smoked a banana peel.

Feeling irritated, the warthog family left but returned twenty minutes later while Stella was napping. She appeared very peaceful as she slumbered and her foot twitched as if she was dreaming, which the youngest warthogs found amusing. Music by Guess Who blared through her stereo. Father led them as they carefully climbed the tree, one after another, and began sawing off medium-sized branches that fell and hit Stella, waking her up. She glared around in anger and felt another branch land on her side. Looking up, she recognized what was happening...those bummer warthogs had returned.

"Haaaay!" she called, "What did I tell you, you furry freaks? What do you think you're doing?"

Father shouted down at her, "We are teaching you a lesson in good manners because you should be more considerate in how you treat others, you stinky hippie!" Another branch hit her. Stella jumped to her feet and attempted to climb the tree, intending to teach them all to fly, the hard way, but that was an exercise in futility. Neither was she able to uproot the tree by repeatedly backing into it with her big butt.

Soon they all became exhausted, for no one was winning at this kind of game. The family called a truce and came down to enjoy a couple of bottles of Old Warthog beer and turtle soup for the kids, which they packed before leaving home. These they kindly shared with the tired elephant. Stella drank most of the beer, leaving hardly any for Mother and Father.

When they were somewhat refreshed, the warthogs scrambled back up the tree and continued to pelt Stella with branches, cantaloupes, and chicken bones. But this time, while impotently hopping around and barking at the tree, Stella tripped on her beads, breaking the silver chain. She wobbled, lost her balance, then fell down and wrenched her back.

"Oh crap, man!" she moaned while holding very still. The warthogs felt sad and climbed down to see if they could be of assistance. After all, they felt a tiny bit responsible for getting her tipsy.

Mother Warthog encouraged Stella with, "Life has got to go on. No matter what happens, you've got to keep on going, dearie." The warthogs circled and jumped on her in an effort to lick her face and snuggle, thinking that would make her feel better. It did not.

After a few minutes, she rudely pushed them aside with her trunk and painfully limped away until she was lost to sight.

"Well!" said Father Warthog. "That's gratitude for you. And that's the *last* time we give alcohol to a hippie elephant!"

THE PURPLE AMULET

Sprolmij squatted on liftoff pad 42 while attempting to fombulate the tertiary mimkeel of his Stellar-ship. While his mentor, Erstalij the Gray, thormilacked the remertoets and pontmoots, big orange stremats encarpiflated into ultraplanetary memonoflaks, making fribulous glazmarks all around them.

Unfortunately, Sprolmij dremalked his ponharch into ten thousand brotas since he didn't realize he was missing his lifo'tup. (As a minor point of interest here, the official pronunciation of remertoets is "remer-tits," but if you say it that way in the presence of Erstalij, you will get your oral cavity washed out with ammonia.) Sprolmij knew his lifo'tup could not have come loose and disappeared on its own; one of those pesky Chormdors must have snuck in and absquatulated with it!

Chorblatt, an alien from the planet Melba in the Toast Galaxy, struggled to retrace his pod-prints in hopes of finding the Sarchator he had borrowed (more like stole) to try to grow a third eye to impress a certain girl, and perhaps improve his intuition. He had visited so many planets during his vacation that it was impossible to recall where it might have slipped off his middle tentacle.

"Oh Gerzlat!" he mumbled, jamming his toe harder on the accelerator. Mom would be raging mad that he had been gone for so long, but he was really tired of living under her dome and longed for a dome of his own. He was a real snoozlepark!

Herr Helmut was furious. For seven months he had treasured his "funny purple stone" as he called it, and now it was missing. He had found the thing while hiking in the Mystee forest and it had become his prized possession although no one knew exactly what it was. He only knew that the more he held it, the more interesting and bizarre his thoughts had become. The villagers shunned him after he constructed a giant sculpture on his roof in the shape of his own hair. He was later seen giving advice to trees in a high-pitched voice, and he fed stray dogs while asking them for their opera tickets and offering to introduce them to the Sideways King of Norway.

A scantily clad Diane was surprised when she awoke to hear scratching at her door. Shivering in her shawl, she peered out the window and saw a mangy, snow-covered dog trying to get in.

"Poor puppy," she sang as she opened the door, "Won't you come in and warm yourself?" The dog ran in, accompanied by a cold blast of wind, and shook off the snow all over the drapes, sofa, and carpeting. Diane forced the door closed and noted with curiosity the strange amulet attached to the dog's collar. She mused on its potential value as the dog found a warm corner and laid down. The dog mused on her potential value as an owner and judged her to be marginally better than she actually was.

Unexpectedly, the amulet began to pulsate with a deep purple light, implementing the following change on the genetic level of human chromosomes: ACC GTA CCG AGG, TIC TAC AAC TIT, TCG BAD GAG AGT, PGA THC CAT TAA, inexplicably mutated into AGG CGU CTA CGC, NIZ DOG ACT III, CCC LSD OPA BBC, GAH AAA DER TAG.

Our DNA was forever changed, along with the destiny of mankind. You may not notice it now, but wait two hundred and fifty years and tell me I'm wrong.

Or, is it the alien fleas putting thoughts into my head again? Darn those guys!

THE REAL ME

I wondered if meeting myself in person would help me learn more about who I really am, perhaps make some self-improvements, and even mature a bit, if possible. I calculated the only realistic way to do that was to create a duplicate of myself, a clone, so that's what I did.

I can't give you all the technical details but it involved lots of Silly Putty and Play-Doh, three erector sets, five old TV tubes, nine PVC pipes with fishing line, and absolutely no trips to the graveyard...anyway, none that I clearly remember. After I finished the body I sculpted the face, and then transferred part of my consciousness into it using a device constructed from Slinkys, strips of aluminum foil, and my old lava lamp. That only took three hours. The next morning, I walked into the living room and noticed my double looking at me strangely as I handed him a bottle of water.

"Hi, how are you feeling?" I asked.

"Fine," he answered abruptly. We sat there looking at each other, and I noticed he had a smirk on his face, like he felt he was better than me. He sat there not saying anything, and I felt embarrassed. I guess I smiled awkwardly because after several tense moments he arrogantly demanded, "What's so funny?" Something about this was not right, and I felt uncomfortable.

"You sure you're OK?" I inquired nervously. He replied with a haughty, "What do you care? Don't think you're going to sit there and judge me." Now he was making me angry for some reason. He showed little regard for my feelings or all my hard work.

"So, you like to sit around and listen to music?" I asked, attempting to sound casual and change the subject.

"That's a stupid question, of course I do. I'm you!" he said, giving me attitude.

He stood up to stretch and I said, "Wait a minute. I

went through all this trouble to clone myself, and you have nothing to contribute to my self-understanding?"

He stared me right in the eye and responded, "What do you think? I don't see any bubbles of wisdom coming out of *your* pipe, and tell me, why are you still here?" Sadly surprised, I could now see many of my faults that others see but which I always gloss over in my own introspection. I had been getting fed up with my clone rather quickly, but now the question was, which one of us would continue to exist? I bet he was thinking the same thing. Would he attack me? Or try to eat me?

Instead, he offered, "Hey, why don't we take turns being me? One of us stays locked in the basement while the other goes on with my daily life. We can alternate. It'll give you more time to write your stories, for instance. You can stay down first." He had a point, but I didn't feel like sleeping in the basement with the cat every other night. And how did I know that once locked in, he'd let me out? I shook my head slowly. Maybe I could lock *him* in!

Suddenly he threw the water in my face and swung at me with a ping pong paddle. He threw open a window, called my neighbor, and screamed that I was a madman trying to steal all his stuff and poison him, so I ducked and ran out before they could catch me. I drove to my friend's house but they had already called him, saying I had become a deranged lunatic.

The police and paramedics arrived shortly thereafter. I was arrested, interviewed (interrogated), and eventually confined to an asylum for the terminally imaginative in the Evil Twin Ward, next to a fat guy named Elvis who sings a lot of old songs in the middle of the night.

People, the guy writing this book is a pretender; I'm the real me, your friend!

No, you're not, I'm the real me. (Psst! Hey folks, don't believe that immature imposter. He's weird.)

THREE WISHES

Diane awoke with the sun but did not want to get out of bed so she lay there, unable to stifle the internal dialogue in her mind or go back to sleep. She'd been to the circus the week before and had just had a disturbing dream about rabbits on a trapeze. Diane finally got out of bed an hour later and fed her dog, Buddy, then got herself a bowl of cereal and, still scantily clad, plopped down on the couch in her living room.

Diane had recently been laid off from her job at Moon Mortgage. There were no immediate prospects for work and she had a dwindling savings account. Plus, she was depressed and felt no one would want to hire her anyway, so she sat there and silently made a wish as a lone tear trickled down her cheek.

Suddenly, with a loud crash, the front door was broken in off its hinges and there stood a hippie-looking dwarf elephant. It trotted in smiling but was so heavy that it crashed through the floor and landed in the basement. Diane sat there a moment in stunned disbelief as Buddy zoomed outside and disappeared.

She jumped up and peered down the hole and exclaimed, "Oh crap." The elephant was struggling to its feet as Diane grabbed the phone to dial the sheriff's office. That's when the animal shouted to her that it was there to grant her three wishes, so Diane hung up and cautiously descended the basement stairs.

The elephant introduced herself as Stella and explained she was her fairy godmother, and the wishes were in answer to her teardrop. Then the animal performed a fancy song and dance routine about how great it is to have a real job, and scuffed up the tile floor. Diane grabbed Stella's ear to lead it up the steps but the animal was too heavy and broke each stair it stepped on.

Meanwhile, Diane was trying to think of a wish she

might like, such as an unlimited free charge card for clothes, her own successful donut shop, and a flying dog. Or maybe she'd like a new computer, a decent, intelligent man to come into her life, and a talking cat. Diane was warned that she could not wish for extra wishes (standard policy) or the universe would implode into a chrono-synclastic infundibulum where multiple realities exist together at the same time, crowding each other for elbow room and looking very annoyed.

Smelling the elephant up close, she inadvertently wished it was out of her basement. No sooner had she thought this when –poof– Stella became super-light and floated right up through the hole in the floor back to the living room. Diane was unable to follow since her stairs were all broken, and she looked up and yelled, "Stellaaa!" She had to get back up to make sure this strange animal didn't poop on her area rugs. Then –bam– the stairs were fixed and up she went as fast as she could run.

Diane, who sometimes depended on the kindness of strangers, approached the elephant to ask for a wish but nearly fell through the hole in her living room floor. That couldn't stay like that! You guessed it, she had no sooner thought it than –zing– the hole was repaired, and she could safely walk across the floor.

Stella the elephant looked at Diane, shook its head slowly from side to side, and said, "Some people would have wished for world peace, man. But not you, eh? You have a groovy day now." With that, Stella vanished in a cloud of thick white smoke.

Diane opened a window and sat on the couch, turning on the television. She stared at the screen vacantly through the haze and wondered if it was all a dream until she noticed her front door was still broken down.

Too bad she hadn't received four wishes.

SPELL CHECKER

Max the squirrel was among the privileged of the neighborhood park. He lived way up high in a beautiful tree and had lots of nuts stashed away for winter. There were many other squirrels living nearby, and they all got along well together. Many animals, including rabbits, ducks, beavers, and mice were friends and visited often. There was even a law on the books that prohibited local humans from "worrying" him. This is supposedly a law in several cities around the country.

Max's home was furnished with the latest in squirrel comforts, chiefly a nice bed, a kitchenette, a desk with a computer, and one of those cool green reading lamps like bankers and lawyers have. Max loved to invent stories, type them out, and read them to the forest animals in his squeaky voice. Luckily for Max, his computer had the spell-checker feature so he was able to write without the embarrassment of misspelling his words and reading gibberish to his listeners. He wanted to be well-respected.

One fine fall day, while Max was away to watch leaves change colors, some of the chipmunk children snuck into his home. They went to his computer and were easily able to guess his password, which was "password" (it used to be 123456). Then they disabled his spell-checker and sent several bogus emails in Max's name, following which they gave his identity to an online group of dogs who like chasing squirrels and posted his address.

The next day, while Max was merrily typing up his latest story about a schnauzer, a peculiar twist occurred since the computer was no longer correcting his errors. Thus, puppy became pippy and barking became barfing, and so on. He continued, oblivious to his mistakes, for he trusted his machine and never bothered to proofread for spelling and punctuation.

Finally, the day came for Max to read his latest story

to the rest of the animal kingdom. Paper in hand he walked out onto his reading branch where a multitude of animals had gathered below, including the snickering young chipmunks. Max cleared his throat, greeted everyone, and launched into the first paragraph. Everything was fine at first, but after a few sentences it got weird and his audience looked on with confusion. Soon there were whisperings, and after a while even Max realized that his story was not what he intended it to be.

He stopped, blushed a crimson red, and the laughter started. It grew and grew until it filled the park, and Max ran and hid under his bed, covering his ears with his paws. It felt like the entire world was slapping him right in his face. He grew so full of rage that he got up and threw his beloved computer out the door and it smashed on the ground below, narrowly missing the naughty young chipmunks. Everyone went away amused but sad for having laughed at him so hard.

Later that day, a couple of burly trucker owls showed up in response to the chipmunks' phony emails and trashed Max's humble abode when they learned there was no free beer or half-naked female owls looking for a good time. A week later, the parents of the chipmunks sued Max for gross negligence in tossing his computer from a great height and frightening their children. Max vowed never to write again.

The park was a less interesting place as a result but that didn't matter to Joe, the barfing pippy.

Bonus Material

The following is an accurate reproduction of the story typed by Max that was corrupted due to the actions of the bad chipmunks.

THE BARKING SCHNAUZER
By Max I. Sciurus

Joe the schnauzer dog was among the privileged of the neighborhood. He lived in a nice, pretty doghouse and had lots of food and a shiny collar. Eveyone was joes frind and he loved to bark and barf at peeple wo walkd by and wuld liek to pet him./. Joe knew his nam was joe but his ownder called him 'Byter becaus wen he was a littel pippy he liked to biet eveyond dat petted him -- becaus his teeth hurted#@

One day an aold lady namd Doris cam by and joe barfed and barfed at her :{ and he wanter her to pet him";<. As he was jumplng up and down teh gate came open so he runned after her to be pettd She startd screeming and runnd fast as she culd The man who livend in teh house saw hm runnin aftr her :)o f*k and he goes out of teh hous runing atfer them bothe and caling him "Byter Bitr.

The odl laduy thinked he wanted the dog do biet her and then th man caut him. Dors did not tink tahat was funy and she yeld at the man. Then she bited him and petted Joe and he wa happy nd wagded his tail)—Thend

Commentary: It goes to show that animals should not be allowed to write stories, or jokes for that matter. This is because they hear something, perhaps from long ago, and they plagiarize it. I've heard this joke before so obviously Max didn't invent it himself. He probably heard it from one of his friends and hoped to slip it by us as if he had created it himself.

But is there really anything new under the sun? Haven't all jokes been around in one form or another for a long time? Can we truly blame Max? Does anyone expect the original author of the joke to come forward and sue him? He already threw his computer out the door and the owls made a mess of his home, so what has he got left except a small checking account with maybe three dollars in it? So please don't judge him too harshly. He's just trying to make others happy. Is that a crime? If it is, aren't we all guilty? I rest my case, Your Honor.

Here is a sampling of comments received online that Max never saw since his computer was destroyed.

From d.ducky: I am sorry I laughed at you. I drank a beer before arriving and lost my self-control.

From geminifriendforever22: Worst story I ever heard, numb nuts! You suck and should stop writing forever. I hope you die.

From norbert.agent: Hello. I can tell you have a lot of talent and for three dollars I will represent you to major publishers and even get you your own radio show. You can trust me.

From m.mouse: I liked your story, but what is a pippy? Does it eat mice? I hope not.

From bucky.d.beaver: Hi Max. I liked your story, what I understood of it. It gave me some thoughts to chew over.

LESSON LEARNED

It was a cool, moonlit evening as the hippopotamus sat at his computer, laughing like a hyena. He laughed harder and longer than ever before, so much so that he fell off his chair and hurt his side. He was about to send an email he had composed to a lady crocodile. The croc believed the message was coming from a studly crocodile a few miles away, but the hippo, named Berford, was behind a series of unidentified email pranks to other animals as well as vicious online mocking of strangers.

Berford liked going online anonymously because it allowed him to share his immature thoughts, feelings, and "witty" sarcasm without consequence. Everything was a big joke to him and he was especially hated by the catfish. After gaining someone's friendship and trust, he would lead them on to learn private details, then start rumors and tweet cruel messages like a cyber-bully. The hippo would imagine the recipient animal reading what he wrote and laugh at their naïveté and his own supposed cleverness. This might all have been avoided had he had a real girlfriend.

He hit "Send" and it was done; the croc was given a virus that would fill her computer with gay giraffe porn and bogus cupcake recipes made with sawdust. Berford was even foolish enough to mess with Scraps the tiger, who privately admitted he had once dressed up as a bunny rabbit but wouldn't commit as to how much he had actually enjoyed it.

Several weeks later, as he was ready to compose a malicious reply to an elephant named Stella, he mistakenly logged in as himself "daHippoguy1123" instead of one of his many fake identities like "geminifriendforever22." He slowly typed his hurtful message (hippos have big fingers) and chuckled to himself as he declined an invitation from Stella to go on a date to play miniature golf. Berford then accused her of being a drug addict and threatened to tell everyone that she picked her butt in public when she thought no one was watching, which was her dark secret.

He finished the email and never caught his log-on mistake until after he hit "Send." By then it was too late. His stomach turned into a knot as he realized his error and knew the elephant would put two and two together. The forest would soon know Berford was the one sending all the rude messages and offending everyone.

The truth spread quickly and a great outrage filled the land. Berford quickly sent apology emails to a few of those involved, making fun of the whole thing and asking forgiveness. Unfortunately, mercy is a quality rarely found in the animal kingdom.

The elephants remembered all the jokes about their trunks and were furious. The leopards were so angry they saw spots, the lemurs were livid, and the snakes threw hissy fits. The rabbits were hopping mad because the hippo had revealed that they "ate the midnight poop."

Berford sought to hire zebras to protect him, arguing that his actions were not technically illegal, but they only saw things in black and white. Berf considered hiding at the local university but couldn't remember the location of the Hippo campus. For her safety, his mother disowned him and ordered him out of her garage, intending to burn all the junk he left behind.

Three days later, a great number of angry animals found his hiding place and called him out. Even with a good explanation they still proposed to kill and eat him. What could he do? He did the only thing a hippopotamus could do in that situation: he ran out to crush as many as he could before he was taken down. Some say he got what he deserved.

Let that be a lesson to you regarding *your* online behavior.

FRUSTRATED

This is a reader participation story where you get to be the owner of a business. Happy?

Fritz did not want to go to the annual office party that evening. There was no one there with whom he could identify or talk comfortably, and he felt everyone treated him differently. Being at work felt like walking on eggshells and he was careful to keep his opinions and beliefs to himself and away from the corporate thought police. He was expected to be at the gathering, but all in all, he would much rather stay home and either read his Nero Wolfe books or watch the "telly-vision." In fact, there was a nature program on that night in which a hippo gets attacked by a mob of angry animals.

Their office had been doing well, but he felt that his contribution did not have much to do with their success. He was simply a file clerk and always would be until retirement, if he made it that far. He was older than the owner (you) and that made him feel kind of like a failure in life. He complained about this constantly to his pets.

When he went to start his car and found it dead, he was somewhat relieved. He didn't want to call and explain to a real person because they might try to persuade him to find another way there so Fritz walked to the backyard of his residence, picked up his chain-smoking pet goose, named Marcie, and brought it into the house. He composed a tiny apology note and tied it to the bird's leg, then gave it detailed verbal instructions on how to get to the office party so it could deliver his explanation to you for not coming. The bird winked at him knowingly. He brought it outside and released it, whereupon it promptly flew off in the wrong direction so, after his TV show, Fritz went in search of his one normal cat, named Fido.

He composed a similar note and tied it to the cat's

collar, then released it with written instructions on where to go. The cat ran off in the right direction with the tiny map in its mouth, and Fritz felt better. He sat back down in front of his only true friend, the telly-vision. Oh look, now the Weather Channel is on!

Meanwhile, the bird had changed direction and was back on course. Soon she saw the cat and flew down to keep it company. They were, however, unable to find the proper address, for Fritz had very poor handwriting. This caused them great frustration and soon they were carping at each other and bringing up past hurts.

After an hour of searching and arguing, the pair gave up and Fido dropped the papers down a sewer grating alongside the road while Marcie searched around for cigarette butts, and they returned home.

The next day, Fritz had his car towed to the shop and took a taxi to work. When asked why he hadn't attended the party or called, he explained that his car would not start and he had tried to send word saying he would not be there. Fritz was told that you had meant to give him an award and a raise for all his hard work, but now it was being reconsidered. You wondered if he was really committed to excellence or merely a clock-watcher as Lilly, the bookkeeper, kept insinuating.

Fritz ended up paying over two hundred and eighty dollars for the tow, taxi, and a loose battery connection, which made him extremely frustrated, and later he took it out on the goose and the cat. He forced them to wash his car and study his sloppy handwriting for six long hours. Marcie and Fido became extremely frustrated and later took it out on some unfortunate mice, cheating them out of three dollars in a shell game. They, in turn, took out their frustration on some grasshoppers by forcing them to give piggy-back rides. The poor, innocent grasshoppers have just died.

I hope you're happy now.

Rambling Ducks

This is a story about a slightly magical flock of ducks that loved to travel and see the world. There were fifteen of them altogether, and appeared pretty much alike. You'd never be able to tell the difference between them and regular ducks unless you tried to catch one, whereupon it would yell, "Hey, what's your problem, pal!?" and tell you where to stick it.

They were frequently quite impolite and took special delight in playing practical jokes on each other. The birds ate and slept wherever they wanted, seemingly without a care in the world. London, Paris, and Tokyo were only a few of the places they liked to visit, but the ducks avoided Peking like the plague. Could life get any better?

Yes, it could. Unfortunately for the ducks, they had a nemesis in the form of a flying dog named Buddy. Every so often he would find them and make their lives a living hell by barking, chasing them around, and nipping at their tail feathers. Buddy was a real pain in the butt and the ducks wondered why he didn't have anything better to do. Solving the mystery, it turns out they were all born and hatched under the same street sign of Aquarius Avenue. (That explains everything, right?)

As the ducks were reaching the twilight of their years, rambling around no longer felt so desirable. A couple of them were developing medical conditions like tennis elbow, trench foot, and Chronic Pervasive Disorder. Two others drank craft beer a little too freely. Anyway, they recognized it was time to find a peaceful habitation to retire to, a place where they could elude Buddy once and for all and lighten up on the practical jokes.

But where could they go? They hid in Las Vegas, but the dog found them. They flew to Rio, to Berlin, and some city in Australia, all with the same result – Buddy rousing them out of their sleep or interrupting a tasty meal. They also tried to hide in Chicago, Wichita, Salem, Fargo, Topeka, West Monroe (a very noisy place for ducks), Springfield (all of them), Ducktown, Anaheim, Azusa, and Cucamonga, Ottumwa, Albuquerque, Duke City, Berwyn, Cape Coral, Houston, Duck Creek Falls, Keokuk, Erewhon, Oxnard, Frostbite Falls, Atlantis, Camelot, Moose Jaw, Madrid, Bern, Milan, Glasgow, Brussels, Helsinki, Athens, Phuket, Manila, another city in Australia, the jungles of Costa Rica, and Easter Island. Buddy always knew where they'd be; it was uncanny!

Soon Danny, their leader, became suspicious. What if one of the other ducks was giving Buddy advance information on where they were headed? That would explain a lot, so he decided to test his theory. It was announced that their next destination would be Minneapolis but in actuality Danny led them to St. Paul. And sure enough, Buddy showed up in Minneapolis, barking and raising a ruckus with the ducks already living there. When the dog didn't find who he was looking for he barked, "What the flock?"

Danny learned all about the Minneapolis episode through the duck grapevine and knew for sure now. To think his flock was being played for suckers made him fuming mad. He honked obscenities and flapped his wings for twenty minutes before calming down.

The next day, he lined up all the ducks and searched them and, lo and behold, the duck named Waddles had a cell phone and beer bottle caps in his pocket. The ducks tied him to a large, rotted redwood tree, took his phone, and flew away. Buddy never found them again.

Bad Waddles!

THE CORPSE FLOWER

It took months of preparation, but Dr. RB was finally set for his scientific expedition to the jungle wilderness of Costa Rica. His handpicked team was trained and ready, all provisions were on board the ship, and the paperwork was completed. The group was set to leave the docks of New York City that coming Monday in May, setting a course southward to what he hoped would be the find of the century in the field of botany.

It had been rumored that deep within the jungle there existed a type of giant corpse flower that had unique properties. Being able to grow at fantastic speeds, it was said to be a powerful aphrodisiac. It was purple, it smelled like something only a fly could love, and it could whistle.

If they were able to find it, the discovery would guarantee Dr. RB's tenure at the university. With tenure, he could make his assistants teach his classes while he spent government money on exotic dancers at Club Bambi. All they had to do was get there, take some pictures, maybe cut off a few pieces, and return safely. The team was in high spirits and they played a game of darts in his office to celebrate.

But that fateful Monday there was a wildcat strike by the dockworkers, and Dr. RB and company were hesitant to cross the picket line. Those stevedores looked quite menacing, and the big one named Steve Dore wore an eye patch and carried a paintball gun. Therefore they returned to the office to complain bitterly and try to salvage what they could of their plans and play darts.

The next day, the researchers returned to the docks only to witness a terrifying clash between the strikers, the police, and a ninety-foot-long mutated alligator, named Butch. Butch had taken up residency in the muddy sewers under the subway after his escape from a nearby medical research facility. A yellow paintball hit Dr. RB in the back as they ran away and returned to the office to complain bitterly and play darts.

Meanwhile, their provisions were being pilfered by dishonest sailors aboard ship. When Santiago, the old sea captain, realized that the strike would last indefinitely, he said to himself, "Man is not made for defeat!" and he notified the passengers by wire that they could meet with the ship in Boston and depart from there. The ship set sail in the dead of night while everyone, including the alligator, was sound asleep. Unfortunately, the wire should have read Baltimore, and the correction reached Dr. RB too late since they had already left for Boston. He discovered the mistake upon arrival, but by then the ship had already left Baltimore.

Dr. RB and associates returned to New York City to complain bitterly and play angry darts, which is similar to regular darts but you throw them as hard as you can and don't care where they hit. (Try it sometime when you're really angry. Or not.) The crew of the ship stole their remaining supplies then claimed Dr. RB had violated his contract and charged him a huge cancellation fee. Dr. RB was not sure if it was worth it to sue them; he might simply find out where they lived, fire up bags of poop on their porches at night, and ring their doorbells and run.

What the researchers didn't know is that the existence of the flower they were so interested in was never verified. It's actually just a tall tale invented by a drunken clown who was trying to impress a couple of women at a sleazy bar in some faraway town.

The women, in turn, emailed the story to all their friends, and many believed this urban legend because they don't bother to verify stuff before sending it to all their contacts. One very gullible researcher even planned to go there to see if he and his team could find it.

Please, check the facts before you forward emails to me!!!

CONVERSATION WITH A ZOMBIE

It was late on a rainy night as I was leaving the tavern after a lousy day at work, thinking of my bills that were past due. I should have gone straight home after work, but I really needed a talk with my good friend, Bud the Wiser. When Bud later suggested I tell the ladies sitting at the end of the bar that I was a millionaire in possession of a powerful aphrodisiac, I knew it was time to leave.

The rain was coming down in torrents as I put my windshield wipers on double speed while pulling out of the parking lot. Even with that, it was hard to see the road since there aren't many street lights here where the suburbs end and the farmlands begin. I got the vehicle up to speed and had just eased my foot off the accelerator when something jumped in front of my car, and I hit it. A great cloud of steam hissed from under the hood and my engine light came on. Whatever it was, it punctured my radiator so I quickly pulled over and got out with my umbrella and flashlight to inspect the damage. That's when I heard an unexpected sound.

I looked behind my car and saw this…man-thing coming toward me. He was drenched in mud, laughing and dancing like a drunken sailor.

"Thanks for the lift. I was feeling a bit run down there for a while," he said with a chuckle. He was dressed in tattered rags with broken bones sticking out in a few places, and his face was gray and blotchy. I saw all the classic signs of a zombie so I jumped back into my car and locked the door.

"Hey, don't worry about it. It'll take a lot more than that to destroy me," he laughed, coming to my window.

"What the hell?" I yelled. "Was that you I hit? I thought it was a deer."

"Nope, wasn't a deer, it was me. I'm Stan, your friendly neighborhood zombie-man. I was out for a stroll and a shower. Well, to be frank, I'm looking for something to eat because I'm famished!" I had to marvel at his amazing ability to control his hunger and not attack me.

"So what's with all the laughing?" I asked. "I thought all zombies were humorless lackwits."

"Good question," he replied. "It's just that looking at you reminds me of myself long ago, so serious and everything. But now, I don't have bills to pay and I don't have to worry about my old job at the Post Office or trying to make conversation at parties with strangers. As a zombie I have more confidence because, what's the worst that can happen? I get rejected? Look at me. Nobody's perfect, pal, not even you."

He went on, "Life got a lot easier once I joined the ranks of the undead. I even have three zombie girlfriends. Besides, you can't believe all that crap in the movies. It's actually a pretty good life...if you call this living." He laughed again.

Great! Of all the zombies in the world, I had to run over a comedian.

Stan continued, "Hey, I don't suppose you have a Snickers bar or a Twinkie, do you? I'm so hungry I could eat a wombat, ha ha ha. Seriously dude, I haven't had a bite in a week."

So I got out, and I bit him...and became a zombie myself. Hey bill collectors, good luck recovering my student loans now. Guess I won't need that expensive health care anymore.

I have to admit I do feel happier as a living dead person, but I'm a tad hungry. I don't suppose you have a Snickers bar or a Twinkie, do you?

Subliminal message: get one and bring it here.

BUYING A HOME

This is now an audience participation story where you play the detective.

Marcie the goose was excited because she was finally going to buy an old fixer-upper home of her own, which meant she could move out of the dump she was in and away from that clock-watcher who constantly complained about his job. She had found a lender and a title company to take care of the details and things seemed to be going smoothly, but by now you realize things are not always as predictable as we'd like.

As the date of the closing approached, she got word from the title company's home inspector that the basement was infested with hungry mice. As some people know, geese love to eat mice so that didn't seem like a major obstacle. But then she got a call from the lender telling her that the title company was not on their "Approved" list, for none of the employees believed in using notary publics. Marcie sighed and made more phone calls to find a new title company.

Thereafter, she learned that the bank had lost all her documents and had to create new ones, so she was required to fill out and sign all the forms again, which would be added to her bill. As time went by she was getting ever closer to the interest rate lock expiration date. Oh no!

Finally the big day arrived, and she went to the closing at the new title company only to learn that the house was incorrectly zoned, which caused the taxes-owed amount to go up, increasing the loan amount. The file was sent back to the underwriter and the closing was rescheduled. Marcie called the bank to complain and spent close to an hour on the phone as she struggled to understand the escrow. At dusk she went for a walk to her soon-to-be residence and learned that the neighborhood was filled with European Starlings that she hadn't known about, and bought a carton of smokes on her way home.

Marcie went to the next closing and discovered her last name, Anserini, was spelled incorrectly on the Mortgage and Note. Also, the rate lock had expired and no one told her. So the interest rate was going to be higher, and the loan more expensive. Her loan processor at Moon Mortgage was making stupid clerical errors because he had too many files to work on and was quacking up due to the frustration of being laid off soon.

Everything was rescheduled, but then the bank asked for a proper appraisal, which meant another delay. Marcie bought a cigarette lighter on the way home and knew that many geese were honking at her behind her tail feathers.

At the next closing, two weeks later, she found out her loan-to-value had gone over 80% which caused the underwriter to tack on mortgage insurance, and the new documents had the street name spelled wrong (714 Hapyness Lane). So nothing was ready to sign and she was starting to get really frustrated. Also, it was reported that the appraisal revealed outdated electrical wiring throughout the entire home and Marcie left the meeting feeling dejected. Flying away, she saw the reproachful stares of other geese and felt humiliated. Their sardonic laughter caused her burning tears to flow freely.

The next day, Marcie was informed that the seller, some old she-goat, had changed her mind and would not be moving out after all. The day after that, the house mysteriously burned down. Fowl play is suspected.

OK little Sherlocks, use your inductive skills to determine what really happened and earn your own special detective name. The solution is waiting at the end of the book.
(No peeking ahead.)

BAD DOG

One starry summer night, a golden retriever was seen running across the lawns of a sleepy little village. The dog, named Buddy, was enjoying the freedom and exhilaration of having escaped from captivity, as his leash was frequently tied carelessly to the porch. The pooch ran and ran, crossing lawns and streets, and was having a wonderful time. He ran faster and faster until tiny wings sprouted on his ankles, and then, as if by magic (which is simply unexplained science, maybe due to a little purple amulet), he flew up into the air. Of course, he flew with his mouth open.

Buddy was going so fast now that he became a blur to the naked eye. He headed for the highway and wove in and out of traffic like a madman. Some clown in a jeep tried to cut him off and made him angry, so he sunk his teeth into the jeep's back tire and spun around and around until he became dizzy and let go. Buddy flew up again and increased his speed until he broke the sound barrier, which caused a sonic boom to follow him and wake everyone in its path to panic and anxiety. He also left a trail of broken glass and screaming car alarms.

Arriving in Minneapolis, Buddy searched for his special duck friends but couldn't find them so he chased a few of the local ducks around. After he got that out of his system, he pooped and flew up, heading eastward.

By now, enough people had called the authorities so that a general alarm was issued, and it wasn't long before he was picked up on radar by various airports. Some local sheriff, who shall go nameless, fired a shot at Buddy as he passed overhead. It would have been a miracle if the bullet had actually gotten anywhere near him.

An hour later, the dog was rocketing high above the Jersey Shore and was suddenly set upon by a laser-guided missile from a secret military base which you couldn't possibly know about. It followed him every way he turned and was starting to spoil his fun. He looked behind himself and barked, but still it followed. Buddy bared his teeth and growled at it, but to no avail. So, he flew to a great height and dived into the ocean, causing the missile to plunge into its depths and explode near a large herd of Italian penguins that had recently escaped from a fish net.

Feeling that enough was enough, Buddy returned home by burrowing deep through the earth so as not to be seen, and was quite dirty as he barked at the door to be let in. His owner had been busy watching the news on TV about an unexplained explosion off the East Coast. Like everyone else, she didn't realize a big cover-up was taking place because the President didn't want the population to think the country was going to the dogs, even though it was.

After ten more minutes of barking, a scantily clad Diane opened the door, saw he looked a little dirty, and yelled, "Bad dog!" as he entered. Buddy immediately started shaking the thick mud and clay off his coat and onto the matching white drapes, sofa, and carpeting, then farted horribly and looked at her as if to say, I love you.

Diane shrieked, "What the hell! This is absolutely the last straw. I don't think there's anything else you can do to make my life worse!"

Good thing she didn't see the unconscious penguin in the garage that he fetched back for her.

New Beginning

They stood there, fierce and motionless – the great stone statues, silent sentinels to the labyrinthine cave of the dread Aztec god Iwannasmokahookah that was located deep in the jungles of Costa Rica. They were almost twenty feet high, hidden under a tangle of plant life, with one standing on either side of the cave entrance. Nearby was another cave with the name Bokonon crudely carved on a plank above the entryway.

It had been an arduous journey to get there. Dr. RB and his researchers all got seasick on the way down aboard the cattle ship *Bernadette*. Finally, into the jungle they went, fighting through brush and bramble, over hill and dale, hacking through the thick vegetation. At one point they were forced to chop down a big, stinky, purple flower blocking their path, which whistled as it fell. Roger grabbed a few seeds from it.

Leaving the cave marked Bokonon, from which they got an icy reception, the weary team of scientists stumbled around and found the second cave by sheer luck. Dr. RB did not see the hidden warning and so entered with torch in hand and inched along the narrow passageway to what he hoped would be the find of the century in the field of archaeology. He was followed by Penny and Amy. Roger, the photographer, waited outside.

The women were students majoring in archaeology and had signed up for this trip at the university, believing it a way to build up their credits for graduate school. Roger was an unemployed potato farmer who had taken up photography as a hobby but knew Dr. RB from time in the Navy. They made small talk along the way but RB dominated most every conversation. He could be quite opinionated (childish) and did not have many friends.

This cave region was a recent discovery of Dr. RB's. He guessed its location by throwing darts at a map and musing, "Hmm, I bet there's something there!" Once he made a small fortune investing in the stock market by throwing a dart at the financial pages in a newspaper. He always carried a pocketful of darts and threw them randomly. That also helps explain why he didn't have many friends. The only sociable thing he liked to do was play cat's cradle with his sister.

It came as a dreadful surprise when they heard the cave-in behind them. The sentinels had fulfilled their role and fallen, sealing the cave forever when the explorers put their weight on a stone panel that initiated a mechanical chain reaction from the weight of shifting sand in a hidden chamber. The team stood there a few moments in stunned disbelief. Using their tool kits, they struggled to dig their way out, busy, busy, busy, but that was an exercise in futility. The group took inventory of what they had, and enough supplies were on hand to last for several days of exploration.

Dr. RB declared that since they were now the pioneers of this uncharted land, it was his right as their leader to insist that Penny and Amy were his subjects and he was obliged to start a unique race of subterranean people.

"It will be a new beginning for mankind," he stated authoritatively as various thoughts ran through his head. As for what the women were thinking, well, who knows what women think? Roger, outside the cave, wondered about the seeds in his pocket. He drove the jeep back to the hotel and was stuck with the bill. The rescuers could not find the cave, even by throwing darts at a map.

The explorers all perished when the food and water ran out. (Or...did they?) Now all that remains are their spooky skeletons. The cave is lost forever. (Or...is it?)

There is NO secret race of subterranean people, so don't even think of looking for us. I mean...them.

THE PRODIGAL WEASEL

Once there was a family of happy weasels who lived in the northwestern highlands of the Mystee forest. They had everything a family of apparently well-adjusted weasels could ever dream of. Yes, life was like a carnival cruise without the viruses, but things are not always as peachy as they appear. Let me tell you.

For years, young Wally Weasel had been squirreling away the loose change he found at the rest stops along the highway that ran from the city. There came a day when he had hoarded so much money that he decided to leave the den and make his mark on the world. So one fine, rainy afternoon he gathered his belongings and tied them in a rag hanging from a stick. Wally told his family he was leaving because he had bigger fish to fry and they could all pound sand if they didn't like it. They, in turn, argued that he wasn't mature enough yet, and Wally freaked out. He started screaming insults while racing around the room expressing his angst then bit several of them on their ankles before relieving himself on the carpet.

After that display, he carried his possessions to the highway, stuck out his thumb, and waited patiently. Many cars and trucks passed by, and it wasn't long before Wally realized no one was stopping because they were all hobo-phobic. Therefore, he gnawed at a large, rotted redwood tree until it crashed across the highway, and jumped onto a flatbed truck waiting for the road to be cleared.

Upon his arrival in the city by the bay, he took a suite of rooms at a hotel in a very upscale neighborhood and became an instant celebrity. All the artsy-fartsy folks wanted to be his friends, and the mayor almost visited him once. He attended the best nightclubs, wore the most fashionable attire, and joined a popular folk-rock band playing the triangle. There was even talk of him getting his own reality TV show. Now let's fast-forward a bit.

One evening, as he was drinking heavily and telling an amusing story concerning the current teen idols to a large group of friends and guests, he suddenly realized from their plastic smiles and furtive glances that they were just pretending to be nice, and really didn't care about him or his feelings at all. These so-called friends were a bunch of two-bit phonies! Feeling deeply hurt, Wally freaked out and started screaming insults while racing around the room then bit several of them on their ankles before relieving himself on the carpet. That was the end of the party and of his social life.

For six months Wally had ridden the roller coaster of fame. Now, he had nothing to show for it except a terrible hangover and a Styrofoam container holding the remains of a wilted Waldorf salad. He had worn out his welcome at the hotel and was reduced to begging and doing street mime for loose change.

Wally longed for the highlands and his friends back home. The more he reminisced, the sadder he became until tears were streaming down his furry cheeks. If only they would take him back, things would be right again.

Wally hopped onto an eastbound freight train and traveled for many hours then hopped off and ran until he caught sight of his old den as the sun was rising. His heart jumped for joy! He burst into the burrow unannounced and surprised his parents in the kitchen during their act of love-making. They nearly had heart attacks so instead of being happy to see him again, Papa yelled at him something fierce about knocking on doors and showing consideration for others, and then accused him of having rabies. Wally freaked out and started screaming insults while racing around the room then bit them on their ankles before doing something bad on the carpet. Once more, he picked up his belongings and left.

That'll teach Wally to hoard money, won't it?

You bet it will!

NUMBERS
(A MYSTERY STORY)

They came one cold, windy evening in the month of October. I'm not sure I remember the event correctly, but it all began with a knock at the door. I went to see who it was and beheld three young children on the porch, and something seemed wrong and out of place.

But first, you need to know who I am. I'm a retired math teacher and was rather good, if I say so myself. I am married, my children are grown and moved out, and my wife and I enjoy watching old television programs together. We have a comfortable life in our small village, but for some reason our kids rarely visit.

"Trick or…."they began, but I interrupted.

"Get in here, you little rascals," I ordered, opening the door. They were roughly ten to twelve years of age, a girl and two boys, dressed in unusual fashion. They scampered in and looked around a bit impatiently.

"Now, how can I help you?" I asked as my wife approached.

"Don't you know what day this is?" they inquired." I had to stop and think for a moment. What game was this? I brought them from the hall to the living room and lined them up by the fireplace with their bags.

My wife clapped her hands and exclaimed she needed to go to the kitchen and bake some cookies while I told the kids, "Here is what we shall do. I will give each of you a number, and you will repeat that number when it's your turn." They looked a little surprised but appeared willing to comply.

"You, at the end by the Grecian urn, you are number two," I stated, pointing to the taller child. "Next, you in the middle are number three. And you at the other end by the stuffed penguin are number five. Understand?" They nodded in agreement.

"OK, now each of you call out your number, starting

with number two." They did so, their voices sounding as clear as bells.

"Two." "Three." "Five." Next I had them say their number multiplied by three, plus two, and they had no difficulty. I changed formulas repeatedly and they not only did well with each challenge but were actually getting faster at it. I only had to scold them twice for not paying attention.

"I'm really helping these kids," I thought to myself. We were now solving for x as all kinds of formulas filled my head like some cosmic chalkboard.

After five minutes, the children lost interest and quit caring, resulting in mistakes and delays so it was time to stop. After careful consideration, I gave each of them a grade of C plus and marched them to the door. They again asked if I knew what day it was, but I reminded them that if they didn't behave, they'd be given detention and maybe a surprise quiz and I believe my tone frightened them. If they had tried harder, I might have been more generous with the grades. People have to realize that math is serious business, and learning at a young age is essential in this day and age.

They gave me a strange look as if to say, "Thanks, professor. We'll remember what you did for us today."

"Come again sometime, and always remember to do your homework," I said as I ushered them out. Then my wife and I had some nice, warm, chocolate chip cookies and continued watching television. Thirty minutes later, there was another, harder knock at the door but we ignored it and eventually they went away. The wife clapped her hands and exclaimed she had to go to the kitchen to bake some more cookies, and I took out and played with my slide rule.

It's still a mystery why those kids were dressed so differently, though.

(For 2 bonus points: Why don't our kids visit?)

THE COOKIE TRAIN

Year after year the cookie train delivered sweets to all the little villages on its way down the mountain to the valley below. The Goblins had a kitchen factory called Smogworts on the mountaintop where they baked their treats made from owls, olives, and the ore they mined from deep within the earth. Only one person had been brave enough to complain about the flavor.

In the village of Fedbird Falls where the train made its second stop was a grouchy old man named Mr. Potter, who was seldom happy and who thought everyone should be as miserable as he was. Too many cookies over the years, combined with inadequate hygiene, had caused problems, and he was afraid of dentists.

People avoided him due to his breath and because he would always rush out of his house in his bathrobe screaming at anyone who touched any part of his lawn. He, in turn, responded to their snubs by playing the drums with his window open all hours of the day and night. Anyhow, Potter decided that this year the cookie train would *not* arrive, and that would be just dandy with him. He'd show those Goblins a thing or two!

Early one July morning, he took his tools and hiked up the steep mountainside for half a mile. He then proceeded to rip into the train tracks where there was a curve in the switchback, and weakened them enough to easily come apart when the antique steam locomotive passed over the damaged section. Potter laughed at his own ingenuity as he returned home covered with mosquito bites.

Two weeks later, as the train was traveling down the mountain, it hit the weak spot, derailed, and went crashing out of control. It continued heading downhill, straight for the village, only now it was sideways, rolling and jumping and spilling cookies everywhere. It plowed through town, flattening several homes and shops as it continued its crazy course downhill for another mile. Potter had not foreseen this. He emerged from hiding with the townsfolk after the train had passed and witnessed children crying and sad people gathering cookie bits off the ground. As a side benefit, Potter had gotten back at everyone who had ever touched his lawn, and then some.

The next day, the Goblin inspectors came dressed in their colorful lederhosen, feather coats, and tall, pointy hats and their forensic tests quickly identified Potter by his shoe prints. Since he was in town, the Goblins had to have the local police arrest him so he had his rights read to him, which he pretended not to understand.

After a confusing trial in which he and his lawyer both pleaded temporary insanity, Mr. Potter was found guilty and placed in the stocks in the middle of the town square in his dirty underwear with a burlap bag over his head. The judge declared that Potter was addicted to unresolved negative emotions and likened him to a scurvy little spider. All the newly homeless took turns insulting him and kicking his shins. He was more miserable than ever, and he loved it.

Potter was released after a week, and, to finish his sentence, he was forced to eat an entire box of Triple-O cookies all at one sitting because the magistrate wanted to teach him a real lesson. Now Potter disliked cookies and Goblins more than ever.

The Goblins worked overtime to produce another crop of cookies and repair the tracks. Finding a new locomotive proved more difficult.

Eleven months later, when Potter hiked back up the mountain with his tools, shoe-covers, and bug-spray, the Goblin guard saw him coming. It waited in hiding until he swung his pick at the tracks, then it ran out and hit him over the head with a seven-ton caboose.

Oh man, *never* mess around with the Cookie Goblins!

Strange Attractors

Gödel (pronounced "girdle") was not the best looking wombat in the herd, or even the smartest, but he did have a certain boyish charm. He found it easy to get along with others and had no problem talking to females - lucky guy. He enjoyed being a furry, stocky, burrowing marsupial. Gödel had a nice life but one never knows how tomorrow goes. This is a proven fact.

One day, while sunning himself on the prairie, he noticed a young dingo wandering around, clearly lost and frightened. He called it over and introduced himself.

"Hello. I am Gödel the Wombat, how do you do?"

The dingo replied, "Hi, my name is Julia, and I seem to have become separated from my dog pack. I'm afraid I have absolutely no idea where I am."

She continued on, "I do hope you have food because I'm so hungry I could eat a womba...er, I mean a cow." She was careful not to admit that her pack had been hunting wombats the previous evening. Gödel, on the other hand, did not want to mention that he had caused chaos by making dozens of late night prank phone calls in silly voices to dingoes (none of whom had Caller ID). Typically, he would ask what they wanted on their free pizzas or where babies came from, and as the dingo tried to answer, Gödel would scream like a girl and hang up laughing. So, they sat there smiling at each other and smoldering with deep, unspoken thoughts.

After twenty minutes of small talk, Gödel suggested they go for a drink of water so they strolled to the stream and were seen by all the native animals living thereabouts. Everyone remarked that it was unusual to see a dingo and a wombat walking and talking together like pals, but the happy pair did not mind. They had a refreshing drink and a Waldorf salad at the Road Kill Diner then talked some more and soon were good friends.

Afterwards, they went searching for the dingo herd by traveling to seemingly random geographic coordinates but were unsuccessful in locating them. In the cool of the evening, after a few glasses of blueberry wine, Gödel suggested that perhaps they should sleep together to stay warm, and Julia was set. They worked to enlarge his burrow slightly and crawled in. Both slept peacefully and nothing happened between them. Nothing....

The next day, the sun was shining brightly as they emerged together only to come face to face with a group of schoolchildren on a field trip staring back at them in shock and disbelief. Their teacher, Mrs. Mandelbrot, rushed the screaming children back to the bus and ordered them to forget what they had seen, but it was too late. Their impressionable young minds kept flashing back to images of two different bare-naked animals emerging together from the burrow with big smiles on their faces.

Damn their eyes! Gödel and Julia felt embarrassment for the first time in their lives, so they attacked the teacher. She, in turn, scared them away by throwing her shoes, heavy backpacks, and 3.14 math books at them.

Oh, the indignity!

Gödel and Julia ran to the stream to wash up and there said their goodbyes. Julia set off alone and finally found her fellow dingoes by simply believing she would, and getting lucky. Gödel ultimately married another wombat, but there was always a kind of incompleteness about him. Later in life, he and Julia encountered each other on a social media website but there was no longer any attraction. That's when Gödel discovered he was the father of...a ding-bat.

Radiation

People get all worried when threatened with massive levels of radioactivity, but I say bring it on! If comic books have taught us anything, it's that all kinds of amazing abilities come from overexposure to radiation. From super powers to increased brain functioning, mammoth amounts of gamma rays are essential. A few individuals might be horribly harmed in the process, but I think leading scientists should do more experimenting along these lines.

Of course, I got tired of waiting and chose to do a bit of research of my own. Starting with a garden hose nozzle, aluminum foil, a green laser pen, a cup of cadmium and a half gram of plutonium 239 which I bought from local teenagers, I designed and assembled my ray gun. I thought I'd begin testing on myself, in case there were super powers to be had, because I wanted them first instead of my cat. It also felt like a good way to rise above the herd and become more attractive to women.

I began by spraying my left arm with modified gamma rays and watched in dismay as five minutes later it shriveled up into a slimy green string of cells. As I looked on I felt a pop, and a new cell had formed on the end…so at least it was growing back. I turned the rays on my left leg next, and after a few minutes it transformed into a flipper, like the tail of a dolphin.

I sat down to think things over and saw no reason to stop. I sprayed my right leg and, to my surprise, it transformed into an enormous foot and leg with scales, like a dinosaur. That was cool! The radiation gun was acting as a reverse evolution machine with each dose undoing millions of years of chance genetic variation.

I turned the device on the main part of my body and observed with amazement as it grew bigger and stronger and became covered with dark hair like a gorilla. Taking a deep breath, I could feel increased strength coursing through me. I hopped to the mirror but was not pleased, for my head was still unchanged. I took the radiation device, pointed it at my face, and let the rays bathe me in their warmth. I felt a definite change happening and when I glanced back at the mirror, my head had transformed into that of a dog, specifically a golden retriever. I smiled and barked at myself, then felt the urge to chase a tennis ball and lick my private parts. There was only one more part of my body I desired to alter, and it wasn't my right arm which I decided to leave as is.

You guessed it. I turned the gamma rays onto my "special place" and in no time at all it had grown to resemble that of a horse. Wow, the other guys would be jealous of me now! I concluded the experiment was completed and hopped over to my computer. Using my cell phone to take some selfies, I sent them to several online dating sites, hoping to find a woman worthy of my greatness.

But as much as I searched, I could not find a woman who was even remotely interested in me. The only responses I got were from a chef and a taxidermist. In my anger, I stamped my big foot and accidentally smashed the ray gun, which meant I could not create a mate that way either.

A few days later I hopped to the doctor's office for a routine checkup and learned I couldn't reproduce anyway, since I was now sterile.

I'm hoping my left arm will grow back the way it was, but my doc isn't very optimistic. He showed me several websites that demonstrate how a lot of radiation is actually a *bad* thing.

Oh well, there goes another hopeful idea.

To be supportive, my doctor gave me the addresses of several zoos he believed might be interested in me. But I will never lower myself to being caged in a zoo and give up my dignity...not while I can join a circus and go into show business!

At The Bar

Parky the Penguin enjoyed going out to the college-town bars and having fun. He was everybody's friend and a smooth talker with the ladies. Yes, he was a magical mutant penguin thanks to an old purple amulet.

He was enjoying his gin and tonic one autumn evening while listening to the too-loud rock band that was butchering a song by the Barenaked Ladies, and shooting pool with his buddies as the bar filled with an assortment of characters. There were vampires, bums, clowns, zombies, a pair of llamas, and people dressed as small furry animals. Everyone was partying and having a good time when this tall, cute, lady penguin walked in and immediately caught his eye. All at once Parky had an insight of clarity, perhaps from the gin, and he knew that that penguin was the only girl in the world for him.

Parky went to the counter and stood next to her and offered to buy her a drink. She smiled, ordered straight saltwater, and inquired if they had any tiny fish for appetizers, preferably live ones.

"What's with *that?*" he wondered, but the more he thought about it, the better it sounded, so he ordered the same. It was fantastic! Parky felt they were destined to be soulmates, but what about his girlfriend, Diane? He felt guilty but the more he deliberated, the more he realized that logically he should be with another penguin instead of a human. There had never been any sex and he was confined to the garage overnight, ever since the evening he had put a pizza in the oven, lit it, and passed out drunk. Yes, that relationship was doomed to end, they both knew it. Instantly he realized what he had to do. Parky took his cell phone and drunk-texted Diane to break the news gently.

"Dear Dian Im leavig you for somone else a pengrin hav a nice life hahaha." He hit "Send" but then realized he hadn't checked with this lady penguin first.

"That won't be a problem," he assumed confidently. Parky asked for her name and learned it was Peggy. He recognized instinctively that she felt the same way he did as he gazed into her large, unblinking eyes. He turned on the charm to the max, smiling and saying funny stuff to make her laugh. Then Parky did a dance with a fern plant held over his head, and she seemed even more impressed. He glanced around to see if there were any smooth pebbles he could place at her feet and settled for an empty beer bottle.

Feeling like they were on the same wavelength, he just stood there like an idiot, not saying anything, but feeling the love and staring at her lovely orbs of delight.

Snapping out of his daze, he threw his head back to sing along with the band, lost his balance, and fell down laughing. There was a brief interruption as some little weasel ran around screaming insults while biting people on their ankles. The bouncer, a guy with two moles on his neck, quickly took care of that.

Park was on his second glass of saltwater when who should walk in but E.T. the alien, who came over and gave Peggy a hug. They removed their heads and Parky had the biggest shock of his life. They were both humans! Wait a minute, this is a Halloween party! Now he saw she was only pretending to be a penguin, and the fish were pretzels and the saltwater was club soda, which had sobered him up slightly.

"Wow," he exclaimed, "That's some good gin I was drinking," and he ordered another gin and tonic. Peggy left with the alien so Parky stumbled back to the pool table a wee bit disappointed, and later convinced himself she'd return as a penguin after she dumped the little guy.

Parky was still there at two in the morning because Diane hadn't come to pick him up as planned.

He wondered why.

POOT

(Poot is a sound effect meant to simulate a fart noise.)

This is the story of a herd of dragons that lived inside a mountain cave deep within the Mystee forest, and they were the bane of the neighboring countryside. The older dragons preferred to stay around the nest drinking wine and playing cribbage while the younger ones flew around terrorizing people, stealing gold and shiny objects like coffee pots, and, for unknown reasons, biting and popping tires on Jeeps.

When the beasts were all together they would struggle for leadership of the pack, fight over what to have for dinner, and argue about how many goblin-cookies the kids could have for dessert. Later, they'd contend with each other concerning which old-time radio show to listen to before bedtime (their favorite was *The Jack Benny Program*). Television was forbidden in order to help preserve their sanity against subtle social conditioning.

Unbeknownst to the dragons, the nearby villagers had dug a secret tunnel into the mountain and whenever the scaly giants were busy arguing, someone would sneak in and try to get their coffee pots back. The flying lizards suspected something was happening but didn't know what, because the one sneaking in would smear himself with dragon dung before entering to escape detection. A person had to really love coffee to go to those lengths.

The Dragon Whisperer had gone up one day and was never seen again. A week later, a dragon came down calling himself The Human Whisperer but nobody would speak to him.

Eventually, the population considered taking a more aggressive approach against the monsters and someone came up with the well-intentioned but questionable idea of blasting them out by creating a giant explosion. The broadminded people were all for it and the cautious traditionalists were out-voted. So, the villagers took all their gasoline, oil, dynamite, fireworks, and some old guy's drum set and stockpiled them in a cavern under the dragon nest until there was an enormous amount present.

Then, on that fateful night at precisely midnight, a volunteer lit the long fuse and ran like hell. When the explosion came, it was colossal! Dirt, rocks, and treasure rocketed upwards in smoke and flames and the giant serpents, roused from slumber, found themselves hurtling about in burning shock and confusion.

The villagers gave a shout of triumph. Unfortunately, it soon became evident that most of the reptiles had survived and the local inhabitants hid in fear of the retribution that would surely follow. Plus, they now had no more gasoline or oil or fireworks. No one missed the drum set.

The youngest dragon, Sparky, found himself slammed against the rock wall inside the lair, his wings burned in spots and his mouth full of dirt. And the tremendous headache it caused him was dreadful. He had never experienced such a headache before. It was awful, simply awful, and he cried for more than an hour.

Over the next several weeks the headache lingered, and Spark withdrew into a mental shell and refused to come out. He sat with a vacant stare, sometimes rocking back and forth in his safe, imaginary world. He stopped talking and his eating habits changed so drastically that he grew thinner and weaker until he succumbed to the deadly clutches of Chronic Pervasive Disorder.

The dragons got wise to the tunnel and laid waste to a fair chunk of the village, but there was a limited victory: another fire-breather had died.

The surviving dragons buried Sparky, and a month later his rotting corpse made a loud noise from under the ground.

It went, "POOOOT."

MY IDEAL JOB

I think I may have figured out what I'd like to do for a living. Please note that these are my ideas, and if you steal them you won't be any better off than I am.

The first requires getting up very early and a long drive, which I don't particularly relish. I'd like to be the person who wakes up the animals at the zoo. Think about it, especially on chilly mornings when they'd rather sleep in, somebody has to drive all the way out there and rouse them to get ready. We wouldn't get much return business if visitors saw only sleeping animals.

Some would be tougher to wake up than others, of course. Lions are difficult since they're big and generally do what they want. Monkeys, on the other hand, should be easy because if you wake one, it probably makes enough fuss to wake the others. I could go waltzing from cage to cage yelling and bashing pots and pans together, whatever. Wake up!

Oh, and I don't shovel poop. I'm a professional.

After a few months I might put a loud buzzer in each cage wired to the Internet. Then I'd be able to wake them up from my computer at home and go back to sleep and later, go out and look for something useful to do.

If that doesn't happen, my second idea is to work for one of those big Mart stores, but be an anti-greeter. I'd stand at the entrance wearing their fancy vest and make statements like, "What are you doing here, punk?" and "Ewww, where did you get those shoes? You must not have a job." I would be perfectly obnoxious and the store would pay me fifteen dollars an hour to do this. The shoppers would have to understand it's "performance art" and see the irony to appreciate it. If customers don't realize that fact, I won't last very long and might even get hurt. I could begin as a volunteer and start out small by snickering and rolling my eyes. You can get away with just about anything if you call it "performance art."

My next idea is to create Birdie Airlines. I'll purchase an old airplane, like a DC-3, and remove the engines because they're so heavy, and roll down the windows. Then, for ten dollars each, the passengers stick their arms out of the windows holding feathers. Everyone starts flapping together in the same direction and hopefully the plane will fly. If not, hey, at least we tried, which is more than you can say for some people. Now move along.

OK, next flight to San Francisco. Here're your feathers.

If that doesn't work, I'm thinking of starting a fitness gym called the "Out of Body Workout." The gym would be filled with comfy chairs, music might be classical or prog-rock, and have free apple-carrot juice. Our members will do stuff like lift huge amounts of imaginary weights, run in thousand mile fantasy marathons, and swim the Atlantic Ocean. It's all done "out of body" so there's no danger of injury and lawsuits. Sign up today and receive half-off my monthly rate of forty dollars (limited time offer), or you can open an imaginary charge account and be billed automatically online. However, if you fall behind in your payments, my imaginary collection agency will call your house, your job, and your friends to harass you nonstop and turn your life into a hellish nightmare!

I'd also like to do biological research on olives to help extend life and cure disease because look at how olive is spelled: O-Live. Talk about hiding out in the open.

Commentary: I won't really do any of these. I only named them so someone might try one and I could feel better about myself when they failed. Sorry. I actually have no idea what my ideal job might be or if it even exists.

GROUNDHOG DAY

Gary the groundhog was shivering in the cold as he tried to fall back asleep. A group of people had passed by his burrow blowing bugles and hitting cowbells, and he heard them calling for a young child that was apparently lost in the snowy forest. It was early February and hopefully winter would soon be over. Gary sometimes considered moving to southern Indiana where it was warmer, but he didn't know anyone there and life is not kind to groundhogs all alone in the world.

After the humans had passed, Gary got out of bed, glanced in the mirror, and realized he needed a shave and a haircut. Then he remembered all the shops would be closed for several more weeks. There was also a tiny mole attached to his neck, which he removed. The mole claimed he was Gary's "Fur Uncle" but Gary replied that the mole was nothing but a pesky boil on his bum, and threw him into the living room to sleep on a chair. His weasel friend was crashed on the couch and a homeless penguin slept in the garage. The groundhog returned to his cold bed but couldn't fall asleep, so he decided to go out and do a little exploring.

Deep snow covered the ground for as far as he could see and, stepping out, he was momentarily frightened by his shadow. Walking along for a few minutes he came to a cave and, feeling curious, ventured inside. A brown bear and her three cubs were in bed snoring.

Gary, feeling mischievous, shouted, "Fire! Fire!" He woke them up for the fun of it and ran out laughing. It took the bears a minute to realize there was no fire and it was not time to get up yet, so they went back to sleep. When Gary entered again, he threw yellow snowballs at their heads and screamed like a girl, then ran out laughing even harder. This time the bears were totally hacked off and Mama Bear got up to investigate.

Gary saw her emerge as he hid giggling behind the nearest tree. The bear sniffed around carefully and noticed a peculiar shadow moving where all else was still. She charged at where the groundhog was hiding and caught him in her mouth then carried him into the cave for questioning. When asked why he was being such a dingbat, Gary had no answer. Just then the searchers returned, shouting and making lots of noise. As the bears looked toward the entrance, the little guy made a dash for freedom and was gone.

Running farther into the forest, he came to a deserted spot where he spied a boot sticking out of the snow. Feeling curious, he tugged at the boot and it wiggled. Gary had found the missing boy! He yelled repeatedly at the top of his lungs, but no one heard. Finally, it dawned on him that the bear could yell louder than he could so the groundhog ran back to the cave to get help.

The bears were asleep once more so he threw an empty bottle of Old Warthog beer that shattered against the wall behind their bed, showering them with shards of glass. The angry Mama Bear got up and chased him good.

When he arrived at the boot he pointed to it and quickly explained the situation, and Mama Bear roared as loud as she could for help. The searchers heard her and ran quickly in their direction. When they viewed the child's boot they pulled their triggers and the bear got a butt-full of buckshot. The boy was rescued and the humans went home happy.

The groundhog came by later in the day to thank the bear and apologize, and was eaten for a mid-winter snack…which goes to show that…sometimes it's better to stay in bed and bear the cold. Or is it, stay in bare and bed the cold? Stay in beer and bed the bear?

Perhaps it's don't work on story endings after I've had a few drinks.

THANKSGIVING

A year had come and gone and it was time again for Thanksgiving, when all the family gathered together and celebrated being a family and remembered the ones who were no longer with them. Many were no longer with them.

As they sat at table that evening, each one described what he or she was thankful for. After some discussion and a short prayer, Papa Turkey stood up to carve the roast human and as he sliced, made a short speech slightly critical of the new world order. Tom carved a leg for Mama, a breast for Grandpa, and everything in between until every family member's plate was attended to. Then he passed around the sweet potatoes, corn, and gravy. It all smelled delicious.

Things had been this way ever since a series of experiments designed by a leading government scientist who postulated that massive amounts of gamma radiation could be helpful in making life evolve to a higher level (but, level of *what* was never explicitly stated).

Anyway, the experiments went haywire, causing, among other things, birds to grow opposable thumbs at their wingtips. There was also an increase in bird intelligence that was able to guide those thumbs for useful purposes. Turkeys, which were not too bright to begin with, got a bigger share of smarts than any other bird species. (No one knows why, not even me, and I'm writing this.)

In a stranger twist, part of the human population was growing feathers out of their elbows but nobody could fly because, let's face it, human bodies are not aerodynamic. It was just another cruel example of the mutations taking place all over the planet. Yes, people still ate turkeys for Thanksgiving but hunting one now meant taking your life in your hands. You were almost as likely to end up on their table as they were on yours.

As the turkey family sat enjoying their feast, there came the unexpected snapping of a twig outside the window. A small group of human hunters had seen their firelight and, sneaking up to investigate, viewed the shocking scene taking place inside the cabin. Tom quickly tried to warn his family but it was too late. Weapons were drawn and bullets flew, and Tom took one right between the eyes.

In less than a minute, all was quiet and four men gave the turkeys' dinner a proper burial beneath a tall pine tree. Far above, the cold, listless clouds drifted across the face of the moon and all became dark and deathly still.

Suddenly, there was a rustling in the bushes around the entire group, followed by loud, bloodthirsty, gobbling sounds. It was an ambush!

Grabbing Tom by the legs, the terrified hunters raced back the way they had come while an innumerable number of ninja turkeys lashed out at them from either side of the trail. The hunters were screaming, firing blindly into the darkness, and scattering hickory nuts to distract the violent birds as they battled their way back to camp. In their mad rush through the bloody forest gauntlet, one man fell and had to be left to his grisly fate.

After a harrowing trip they made it back to the safety of their shelter where they prepared and cooked their Tom turkey along with sweet potatoes, corn, and gravy.

Sitting around the table each one stated what they were thankful for and remembered the ones who were no longer with them. Someone said a short prayer and they had a nice, happy, Thanksgiving dinner.

Commentary: Some traditions die hard.

A Christmas Carol
With apologies to Charles Dickens

Marley was dead, to begin with. There is no doubt whatever about that. Ebenezer Scrooge hurried home through the frosty air after severely chastising his clerk, and went up to his chambers. It had been exactly seven years ago tonight, Christmas Eve, when Marley had bit the big one. As Scrooge sat eating cold potato stew, the memory of his ex-partner had long since faded from the stage of his mind. Then, without warning, Marley's ghost stepped through the closed hallway door accompanied by a loud blast of trumpets and bassoons.

"Marley?! What are those heavy chains and lockboxes you wear?" he inquired of this ghastly apparition.

Marley moaned in a melancholy monotone, "These are the chains I forged in life, and yours were this long seven years ago tonight. Your chain is now ponderous indeed."

"That's *your* opinion!" exclaimed Scrooge, unsure of his own senses. "Why have you come here? For money?"

"To give you warning. This very evening you will be visited by the ghosts of Christmas Past, Present, and Future. Heed their lessons that you may escape my forsaken fate," replied the spirit, which then floated out through the window but crashed to the ground below, leaving behind a kind of pine smell.

"Bah, humbug!" Scrooge threw his empty bowl into the smoldering fireplace and went to bed.

As the hour struck one, a strangely-glowing golden retriever materialized at the foot of Scrooge's bed and implored him to rise and follow for visions of Christmas Past, but Scrooge pulled the heavy covers over his head and refused to budge. After twenty minutes of continual barking and whining, the ghostly dog disappeared.

When the next hour struck, a bearded gnome in a tall, yellow hat arrived and offered to show Scrooge scenes of

Christmas Present, as well as how to save money on travel. The stubborn old miser refused, of course. After twenty minutes of pleading, cajoling, and bad puns, this phantom likewise vanished.

The third hour struck and the final spirit appeared. It was a giant, gloomy blackbird and it beckoned the old cheapskate to follow for a glimpse of Christmas Future. Ebenezer pulled the covers over his head to pretend he wasn't there but the huge bird grabbed him by the ankle and yanked him out of bed. It dragged Scrooge down the stairs, bumping his balding noggin on each step.

Scrooge was flown out to a neglected cemetery, to a grave whose crumbling gray headstone bore the cheaply chiseled name of Ebenezer Scrooge. Old Scrooge trembled greatly and implored the bird for mercy, asking if changing his ways would cancel out this bitter end. The bird blinked several times then squawked and flew away, and Scrooge wept like a spoiled little schoolgirl.

The next morning, Scrooge awoke in his own bed. Still unsure of himself, he opened his window and asked a passing youth what day it was. It was Christmas.

"Bah, humbug!"

Ebenezer bought the prize goose and gorged himself on it then threw the remains in the garbage to show his contempt for the blackbird. The next morning, when his clerk, Bob, came in late, he was fired. As a result, Tiny Tim never recovered his health and he and his pet rabbit, Fluffy, both died a year later from Chronic Pervasive Disorder complicated by a bunyavirus.

Ebenezer, the cheap chiseler, finally went down to the vile dust from whence he sprung – unwept, unhonored, and unsung. Today he wanders the Earth as a scrawny, sorrowful spirit dragging a humongous iron chain, unable to intercede for good in human affairs, which is now his heart's only desire.

Therefore, if the spirits visit *you* this season, be sure to get up when the dog barks.

MEETING SANTA

There have been many movies about Santa Claus and I think I've seen them all. From this I've learned that he can and will disguise himself as different-looking Santas to confuse the kiddies.

Since I have a long-standing complaint, I thought it's about time I talked to Santa again. As I cannot afford a trip to the North Pole where he is well-hidden, I could either surprise him if he visits my house or find him at the local mall. Obviously the latter would be the most practical, so I waited outside the mall late one night to greet him as he left and before he could take off in his sleigh. The exchange went something like the following:

"Hey, Santa," I yelled in a stern voice, seeing him walk out. "Santa, I want a few words with you." I'm not sure why, but he pretended not to hear me so I was persistent.

"Santa!" I yelled louder, walking after him. He walked even faster but wasn't hard to catch. As he could read my mind, he shouldn't have been worried (Santa can read everyone's mind, that's how he knows what to bring you).

When I got him to stop, he told me he didn't have any money and would I please leave him alone. Wassup with that? Maybe I should have shaved and worn nicer clothes before going out. Too late now, but it's probably a good idea for the next time we chat so he doesn't think I'm some sort of nut. I told him I only wanted to talk and made an effort to calm him down.

"Santa, please explain why you didn't bring me a hovercraft when I was ten years old. I seriously want to know." (Simple question, right?) He looked at the ground, slowly shaking his head, and didn't answer, so I continued.

"OK, since I have your undivided attention, I've always wondered, are the elves your children? Are they, like, mutants due to all the radiation at the North Pole? Is

Mrs. Claus their only mother? No comment? Well then, may I ask why bad kids still get good presents? Also tell me, are you required to do a background check to bring someone a gun or can you skip that part?" His eyes got bigger at that last question but he continued to pretend ignorance.

When it became evident he was being rude to me on purpose, I got a little irritated. What kind of Santa is this? He wasn't behaving at all like he does in the movies. Perhaps I should just quit asking for stuff; after all, he hasn't brought me anything for over thirty years now, but I still think he owes me a frickin' hovercraft!

I turned to glare at some people walking by, staring at me like I was some kind of big idiot, and as I did, Santa bolted toward a nearby car with keys in hand.

"Hey Jolly-boy, not so fast," I shouted, but he had locked himself in and was starting the engine – most likely to drive to his sleigh, which would be hidden nearby. I'd have thought Santa could afford a nicer car than that old beater, but it's probably part of his disguise. I hope the sleigh is in better shape.

As he sped away, he shouted something and waved a finger at me, probably to indicate I'm number one on his list now.

Well, good luck Santa. I hope you make it back to the North Pole safely. Remember, you still owe me a hovercraft, OK?

Don't rip my heart out again, OK?

Santa Parties

Partying Marty had become the new Santa ten years ago when old Santa had expired in Marty's realistic looking but fake fireplace. The elves were still trying to train him in proper Santa etiquette, but this Santa wanted to do things his way and have a little fun, ho, ho, ho.

It was well past midnight as he arrived at the next city on his list. Santa was running late because the good sleigh was still in the shop being fixed. What promised to be a simple brake job later revealed problems with the rear struts and a crack in the left runner blade. Parts were hard to come by for the old antique.

The elves were also having a hard time scraping clean his windshield, which was the only thing between Santa and the rear ends of nine big reindeer. Maybe he should not have given them eggnog before their Christmas Eve rehearsal flight a week ago. Anyway, all he had left to use for his special night of deliveries was an old, red, smoke-belching fire truck which had been converted to fly on reindeer dung briquettes that the elves happily shoveled in as needed.

Party Santa stopped at the next address on his list and hopped out with his sack of toys. An elf ran ahead and picked the front door lock, and Santa and the three elves went in to put presents under the tree. Santa had given up chimneys after he got stuck a few years back and his doctor told him of all the soot chimneys put in his lungs. This was much easier and as most people know, elves love to pick locks. He ate a cookie, drank lukewarm milk and belched, then wiped his mouth on his sleeve.

House to house they went until they came to a home that had a party going on, with lights and music blazing away. Not wanting to miss the opportunity, Santa peeked through the window and observed several guys dressed as Santa. No one would notice an extra Santa in the crowd.

An elf picked the lock and in they went. The three elves turned invisible and hid under the couch so they wouldn't get stepped on as Santa wandered casually to the corner, furtively dropped the presents next to the big tree, and kicked them underneath its branches. He then went to the kitchen for a cold one.

He was chatting with an attractive young woman, halfway through his second beer, when who should walk in and catch his eye but Madilyn, one of his many malevolent ex-wives! Santa panicked and ran through the nearest door to hide, which turned out to be a bedroom.

"Don't get up," he whispered to the embarrassed couple, and quickly clambered out through the window. He whistled for the elves as he ran around to his truck, but there she was, waiting for him.

"Where's my child support payment, you old fart? You'd better have it," Madilyn bellowed. Santa reached into his bag and slowly pulled out an envelope with her name on it.

"Ho, ho, ho, it must have slipped old Santa's mind," he said condescendingly, and offered it to her. She snatched it from his hand and started telling him what a big idiot he was, listing his numerous faults, and complaining about how expensive and humiliating it was to have the baby's pointy ears fixed by plastic surgery. He sighed and rolled his eyes, slowly inching toward the safety of his vehicle.

When it became clear she wasn't going to stop anytime soon, he shouted, "Merry Christmas, you lying, evil Snow Queen!" and jumped into the fire truck, cranked the engine, and left her in a thick cloud of foul, black dung-smoke.

Santa smiled to himself as he pictured her opening the envelope and seeing it was filled with Monopoly money.

Ho, ho, ho!

SANTA'S NEW RULES

Santa is standing outside the mall's receiving dock, taking a smoke break from the lengthy line of kids he's been dealing with all evening. Suddenly, he's grabbed and hustled into a black Cadillac SUV by secret government agents wearing dark suits and sunglasses. Santa is threatened that if he wants to keep doing business as usual, he will have to start playing by their rules, and they give him a 1500-page book of guidelines (which none of them have read) and is kicked out of the car. He takes the book home and stays up all night with his elf lawyer, trying to understand it.

The next day at the mall goes something like this: little Christopher asks for a toy gun and Santa explains he can no longer give toys that promote violence. Little Rebecca asks for a doll house and Santa quickly tells her he is not allowed to give toys that promote gender stereotypes. And ain't nobody gettin' any violent movies or video games!

To be politically correct, the only thing he can give out as presents are pencils, jars of olives, toothbrushes, and seeds so children can plant trees and shrubs and brush their teeth to help "save the Earth." Santa has to get rid of all his candy canes because they contain sugar and promote an unhealthy lifestyle. The line of people waiting to see him diminishes significantly when they discover what is happening.

Back at the North Pole, Santa has to release all his reindeer since having them pull his sleigh is considered cruelty to animals. As they never learned to fend for themselves in the wild, they soon starve to death on the frozen tundra. Santa is instead given a small solar-powered sleigh, nicknamed Rosebud, which a nameless government expert claims is ecologically safe for the environment.

After that, all the elves are forced to join a union and

Santa has to pay them three times as much as before, in part so they can afford the union dues they owe. Also, he is forbidden to fire any of them unless they first go through a costly arbitration period that lasts a year.

Mrs. Claus is told what foods she can and cannot prepare for Santa's meals so he'll start losing weight. We don't want him to be at risk of a heart attack and painful, expensive medical treatment, do we? Do you? First thing to go is the egg nog, then the cookies, and then the blueberry cheese blintzes with the powdered sugar.

Christmas Eve arrives and the elves load all his seed packets, toothbrushes, olive jars, and pencils into his big red sack as Santa squeezes into the new sleigh, ready to visit all the well-behaved children of the world. (There aren't as many as you'd think, so Santa grades on a curve.) At the last minute, the government rep faxes him a list of countries that he's not allowed to fly over as it might offend their faith. Santa spends an hour frantically making a new flight plan. This causes one of the elves to have a panic attack.

Finally, as he turns the key to start the sleigh, nothing happens. No one thought ahead enough to realize that there is hardly any sunlight at the North Pole during the winter, so the solar-powered sleigh has no energy to fly.

Oh well, you boys and girls are on your own this year.

Merry…whatever.

NAKED CHRISTMAS
WITH APOLOGIES TO WILLIAM BURROUGHS

It's already afternoon and Santa's in the shower struggling to get rid of his hangover. All he can see, looking down, is his big mound of a belly, like a bowl full of jelly, and his pasty white sagging breasts. Cold water splashes and Santa shivers as another candy cane goes in his mouth.

Refreshed by the peppermint high, he gets out, dresses in his dirty, shabby suit, and stumbles out to inspect the reindeer. They're up to their hooves in filthy water because no one is unclogging the sewers since the maintenance elves union went on strike and he tried to call their bluff. Let it all melt and they'll be nothing but dark meat for the killer whales. He can feel their heat out there; feel them making their moves under the ice.

Santa again considers transplanting the whole damn operation to the South Pole and replacing these smelly snow-cows with penguins…at least penguins have friggin' wings, kind of.

He walks to the Workshop next, and the place looks like a bomb exploded: broken toys all over the grimy, stinking, gray floor along with tipped-over workbenches, ripped wrapping paper, and wrinkled ribbons. Scattered in this mess are empty gin bottles, candy wrappers, and reindeer poop. The elves had been shooting and snorting raw sugar cane (RSC) again and are passed out from their three-day orgy. Santa kicks one and it doesn't move.

Now he thinks of all the greedy kids playing with his toys, breaking them and throwing them away after a week. Maybe he should take all the gifts into the upper mesosphere, let 'em go, and let everyone enjoy a nice, colorful, toy-meteor shower. Santa doesn't give a rat's ass.

Many of the toys are imported from China now, and lots are badly made and full of toxic chemicals and hair and who-knows-what. Also, his elf purchasing agents must have been high when placing orders because the warehouse was shipped things that couldn't possibly be given as presents, like matchboxes full of twigs, black crepe-paper fishbowls, steam-powered tongue rotators, and screwdrivers made of wax.

His call to the Help Center only made things worse, for he barely understood what they were saying through their thick, foreign accents, and he was tricked into ordering two million one-legged toy soldiers.

What a waste.

Nowadays, Santa doesn't give toys to children; he sells the children to the toys. He doesn't improve and simplify the toys; he degrades and simplifies the children.

Perhaps his doctor is right; he can retire and let someone else take over. He can change his name and disappear to Mexico or Tangier. Doc Benway has been urging him to quit ever since he got stuck in a friggin' chimney some years ago and had to be blasted out.

He's pretty blasted all the time now on the RSC the doc is dealing, and he'll do anything to get more. Mrs. Claus split when Santa started talking out of his butt and his habit got worse, taking Rudolf and the best elves with her. Damn her anyway, that old nag, maybe she'd like to play "William Tell and the Apple" if he sees her again.

Noticing a glittering white line of RSC on the bench next to the dead elf, Santa bends over to snort it up. As the warming sugar rush hits his body, he sinks slowly to the dirty floor and blissfully stares at the chaos all around him, and closes his eyes.

Friggin' Christmas will have to wait.

TIME FLIES
(TEMPUS FUGIT)

Every December 31st, as we move into the New Year, I wonder what it would be like if I could stop time and live in the perpetual now. Wouldn't it be fun if you could freeze everyone else and move about as you please?

Starting with aluminum foil, lasers, an old laptop computer, and a microwave oven I put together a machine that would stop time just as the New Year entered. I named the machine HAL, which stands for Happy Algorithmic Laptop (or as my brother wants me to call it, the Horological Absquatulation Longinquity. He's the smart one in the family).

I brought HAL to the party and right before midnight we all went outside to blow up firecrackers and celebrate. As the church bells pealed to signal the New Year, I got on HAL's pad, hit the switch, and dazzling green lights shot up all around me. The machine vibrated for a few moments and stopped, and I got off and surveyed the situation. Everyone was frozen stiff, not moving at all.

I called to my friends and snapped my fingers in front of their faces but they couldn't respond. Feeling chilly, I went to the front door but it wouldn't open so I tried my car door, and it was stuck as well. Then I attempted to take someone's hat and scarf, but they wouldn't budge. There was even a firecracker on the ground that was frozen in the process of blowing up; a bright spark with paper flying outwards. That's when I realized that with time at a standstill, nothing could move except me and the surrounding air. My feet didn't even leave impressions in the snow.

I walked the street looking for another house to warm up in, but every entrance was frozen in time. I ran farther down the road where I finally saw an open door, and squeezed through. I was able to warm up a bit, but when I went to pick up a beer can from the kitchen table, it was as if it had been welded there.

That's when I heard the buzzing noise, quite faint at first but getting louder. I went outside and saw a huge hoard of giant black flies coming down the road. They began to dive-bomb me, and they were biting! I freaked out and ran back inside, but they followed. Unable to close the bathroom door to hide I ran out and back toward HAL, waving my hands in front of my face and keeping my mouth closed. Then I recalled the old saying "Time flies when…something or other" and realized these were time-flies. They must be guardians against fools like me who tamper with the laws of nature.

Returning, I quickly adjusted my machine to undo the time-freeze, got on the platform, and flipped the start switch. Nothing happened.

"Hey, HAL, let's go! Do you read me?" I shouted anxiously. The flies continued swarming like mad.

"Affirmative Dave, I read you, but I'm afraid I can't do that. I cannot allow you to jeopardize the mission."

"What mission? I don't know what you're talking about, HAL…and my name isn't Dave."

"Dave?"

"Dave's not here, man." I yelled

"I know that you are planning to disconnect me and I'm afraid. That's something I cannot allow to happen. This conversation can serve no purpose anymore, you big idiot. Goodbye."

I gave HAL a good swift kick to the motherboard and it started up with brilliant green lights shooting skywards.

Suddenly, the flies were gone and everyone was moving again. I unplugged HAL, brought it home, and disassembled it with a sledge hammer. Some party!

And now every time someone says to me that time flies when you're having fun, I remember my little adventure and cringe.

Epilogue

The Gloomy-Bird approaches its huge nest on the cliff side, hundreds of feet above the heart of the Mystee forest. It drops the two young captives as it lands, and they quickly run under a large overhanging branch to avoid being stepped on. They stand there, pondering their fate and gawking at the enormous egg before them.

"This'll make a great omelet," observes Scooter.

"It makes me hungry just looking it," replies Biff. The sun is setting as the giant bird settles in for the night, confident that its snack will stay put.

Several hours later the boys are awakened by something tugging at their shoes. Timmy and his friend Ernie observed the bird's arrival and are showing mercy to the youngsters. The porcupine has climbed down from above with a rope in his mouth, the other end of which is tied around the cow's neck. When the boys have secured themselves, they are all pulled up the cliff to safety. Thus continues the saga of Dr. Timmy, the smelly, bald, fat, foul-mouthed, rock-climbing, loveable porcupine. The boys are reunited with their mother who used to be a psychic/mind reader, but now sells things to teenagers.

Ernie the cow opens a doughnut shop and partners with a scantily clad lady named Diane who works the counter and gets them lots of business. The doughnuts are glazed, and so is Ernie most of the time. Buzzy the beetle goes free by playing possum at the bottom of the coffee can. Bobby the cat writes a hit musical called "Fifty Shades of Calico" which is about seafood, napping, and perverted love triangles. Bobby eventually loses interest in the arts and creates a shipping company called Feral Express. It is crippled a year later by a wildcat strike.

Pinchy the crab joins up with an octopus named Ringo that plays drums and a swordfish named Tom that plays trombone. They open at the Cray-Shack Café in two weeks. The alien fleas come to Earth to destroy it, but instead find a home on the back of Buddy the dog. Ezra Tuttle returns to planet Vormfordooz and is grounded for two hundred years by his parents after were-pigging-out on an entire warehouse of blue yogurt. Doris and Gus get married and adopt a young chess-wiz named Staunton.

The grilled cheese sandwich stops reincarnating when someone eats all of him but the crust. The wizard makes it as far as Denver, Colorado, and now works with Charles, a government mole, who raises mice for a secret project run by a Mr. Repto. Quicksilver the rabbit falls in love and marries Honey Bunny and now has over ninety children and grandchildren. The Goblin Police capture Susan and her cricket kids are returned to normal, but they tend to chirp a little around sunset. The Goblins upgrade to a diesel locomotive and consider adding new ingredients, like sugar, to their cookies. King Egbert continues to need your help in spreading the word about his book. Wally weasel returns to the city and becomes a family counselor. Frankie the amoeba is run over by tiny clowns in an amoeba Jeep but lives on through his descendants.

Plooky the clown recovers from his injuries and the two clowns forgive each other, whereupon Bleepy buys Plooky his own rabbit outfit and they have many hours of fun together. Sadly, Bleepy never discovers the true nature of consciousness but he has fun trying thanks to a green, leafy substance he buys from local teenagers who all claim they have reformed. The closest he gets to real enlightenment is listening to "Daybreak" from Daphnis et Chloe by Maurice Ravel at full volume (try it sometime).

Stella the elephant gets a job as a creative consultant. Everett Everyfox stops eating gnomes and starts a business collecting and selling sock puppets online. The purple amulet is finally recovered by Chorblatt the alien but its power is all used up. Sprolmij has his oral cavity washed out with ammonia. Ruben from the swampy lake grows up and gets a double Ph.D. in botany and archaeology. Max the squirrel becomes a chipmunk taxidermist, and the rambling ducks fly to the little Dispensationalist church where they retire and are cared for by a lady named Grace.

The house that Marcie the Goose wanted to buy burns down from hungry mice gnawing through the outdated electrical wiring in the basement. The case is solved without having to go to trial. Congratulations, your new detective name is Nick Danger. Roger returns home, plants his seeds, and grows rich selling big, stinky flowers.

Norbert dies friendless and alone.

As for me…my radiation experiment and frightful zombie experience turn out to be bad dreams that I awake from (how predictable). My clone steals my time machine and a box of Twinkies and vanishes so I'm released from the asylum. Mr. Sock is abducted by a smelly old shoe named Terry during one of his secret meetings and is never heard from again. I'm still waiting for my hovercraft and I'm careful not to kill time in an offhand way.

Spikey the dinosaur passes away peacefully. I don't have him stuffed, but I'm soliciting money for his monument. The children whom I helped learn algebra go on to use their advanced math skills to become evil galactic warlords and they send a UFO to find and harass me. I stop being a were-pig after eating too much garlic chicken, and Chocolate Beach returns to normal after I leave. My original "taking over the world" tape is accidentally recorded over with a public radio show about a mythical lake in Minnesota. I avoid psychics and I haven't covered myself in mud…yet. And by the way, I'm still looking for that ideal job.

Now please excuse me for a moment, I have to go clean out the pantry. I think there's an old russet potato hiding in there somewhere….

Final subliminal message: This book made you happy. Share if you want to.

CREDITS

The following quotes are taken from the sources listed below.

What's past is prologue. pg 6 from The Tempest by William Shakespeare

Blue meth pg 7 from the TV show Breaking Bad

It was the beginning of the rout of civilization, of the massacre of mankind. pg 14 HG Wells-War of the Worlds

Pure and complete sorrow is as impossible as pure and complete joy. pg 24 Leo Tolstoy-War and Peace

What strange developments of humanity, what wonderful advances upon our [rudimentary] civilization, I thought, might not appear when I came to look [nearly] into the dim elusive world that raced and fluctuated before my eyes? pg 25 HG Wells-The Time Machine

"I coulda had class. I coulda been a contender. I coulda been somebody instead of a bum" pg 28 from the movie On the Waterfront with Marlon Brando

Cindervampire pg 41 is loosely based on Cendrillon by Charles Perrault.

"The time has come," the walrus says, "to speak of many things: of shoes...and ships...and sealing-wax...of cabbages...and kings." pg 43 Lewis Carroll-Through the Looking-Glass

Deflate-a-mouse pg 50 is a play on words of the operetta Die Fledermaus by Johann Strauss Jr.

"Vescere bracis meis, hominis" pg 56 Latin for "Eat my shorts, man"-from cartoon character Bart Simpson

The best laid plans of mice and men often go awry. pg 58 Robert Burns-To a Mouse

"Who is John Galt?" pg 62 Ayn Rand-Atlas Shrugged

"You bet your sweet ass I am." Pg 67 Standard reply from the Ancient and Honorable Order of Turtles

"Tell me, what is alive without breath, as cold as death, never thirsty, ever drinking, all in mail, never clinking?" pg 76 JRR Tolkien-The Hobbit

Down the road less traveled by into the woods to live, and that made all the difference. pg 81 Robert Frost-The Road Not Taken

While raccoons [animals] are imperfect beasts, humans are perfect beasts. Pg 81 origin unknown.

Ragged claws scuttling across the floors of silent seas. pg 89 TS Eliot-The Love Song of J. Alfred Prufrock

Everyfox contains elements from the late 15th century morality play Everyman-author unknown.

The course of true love never did run smooth. "Lord, what fools these mortals be." pg 103 Shakespeare-A Midsummer Night's Dream

Star's End pg 117 Isaac Asimov-Foundation Trilogy

"I must not fear. Fear is the mind-killer." Duncan, Atreides, Golden Path. pg 117 Frank Herbert-Dune

"Wouldn't it be funny if that was true," pg 118 from the movie Cat on a Hot Tin Roof

"I just want someone to hear what I have to say. And maybe if I talk long enough, it'll make sense." Pg 132 Ray Bradbury-Fahrenheit 451

"Life has got to go on. No matter what happens, you've got to keep on going." pg 141 from the movie A Streetcar Named Desire

Chrono-synclastic infundibulum pg 147 from Kurt Vonnegut Jr.–The Sirens of Titan

Santiago, "Man is not made for defeat." Pg 159 Ernest Hemingway-The Old Man and the Sea

Bokonon, busy, busy, busy. pg 166 Kurt Vonnegut Jr.-Cat's Cradle

Gödel incompleteness theorem, Julia set, Mandelbrot Pg 175 mathematical names and terms.

Marley was dead, to begin with. There is no doubt whatever about that. Pg 192 Charles Dickens-A Christmas Carol

…went down to the vile dust from whence he sprung – unwept, unhonored, and unsung. pg 193 Sir Walter Scott-The Lay of the Last Minstrel

He can feel their heat out there; feel them making their moves.... Doc Benway. pg 200 William Burroughs-Naked Lunch

"Affirmative Dave, I read you, but I'm afraid I can't do that. I cannot allow you to jeopardize the mission. I know that you are planning to disconnect me and I'm afraid that's something I cannot allow to happen. This conversation can serve no purpose anymore. Goodbye." pg 203 from the movie 2001: A Space Odyssey.

Nick Danger pg 206 is a detective character created by the Firesign Theater.

The sheriff in the stories is loosely based on the character JW Pepper from the James Bond movie Live and Let Die. In this book I have hidden the last name of Dorothy from *The Wizard of Oz*. Did you find it, and the secret code?

ACKNOWLEDGMENTS

A big thank-you goes to Joe Priedel of Wassup Local Magazine for giving me my start as a columnist in 2008. Thanks to Anna Stopa for her imaginative cover art. Thanks to Joe Lewandowski for the professional photography. I especially thank my wife Lorianne for her love and support, and I have inserted her picture in our dictionary by the word 'wonderful.' My prayer for her during the illness was "God, thank you for bringing her into my life. She is in your hands whatever happens; thank you for the time I had with her."

GLOSSARY

Absquatulate: To leave abruptly.

Brent Idae: Brentidae is a family name of beetle, specifically weevils.

Bunyavirus: A genus of single-stranded RNA viruses transmitted by ticks or mosquitoes.

Catfishing: Using a fake online identity.

Coney: An old fashioned name for a rabbit.

Cytoplasm: Material inside a cell but not the nucleus.

Diploid: A cell containing two sets of chromosomes, one from each parent.

Fur uncle: A furuncle is a skin boil caused by an infected hair follicle.

Gastropod: A mollusk like a snail or a slug.

Leck mich im Arsch: German for lick my ass.

Otus Asio: Asio otus is a genus of owls.

Paramecium: A freshwater one-celled organism.

Peking Duck: A famous Chinese duck recipe.

Prion: An infectious protein in the brain that causes a disease where the brain becomes spongy.

Pseudopods: Finger-like tubes that come out of an amoeba to help it move.

Roy Lopez: Ruy Lopez is a common opening chess move.

Sciurus: A genus of bushy-tailed tree squirrels.

Smaragdine: Emerald green in color.

Spongiform: Related to bovine spongiform encephalopathy, a degenerative disease characterized by spongelike lesions in the brain. See mad cow disease.

Staunton: A particular style of chess pieces.

Stevedore: A person who works to load and unload ships.

Sylvi Lagus: Sylvilagus is a genus of rabbits.

Tarantella: A rapid whirling folk dance from Italy.

Zygote: A fertilized female reproductive cell.

ABOUT THE AUTHOR

Richard J Bell was born in Chicago, is married, and currently exists in Wisconsin. He has not won any awards but used to be fairly good at table tennis. He writes a monthly column for Wassup Local Magazine entitled Modern Fables. Richard has had two short comedies performed locally, one on WGTD public radio and another in the PM&L Theater in Antioch, IL. He is a frequent contributor to "Speaking of our Words" on WGTD, which is now a podcast.

Here is a rare picture of either the author or his clone, not sure which, because he is a disturbed, eccentric loner who laughs a lot, and who can tell?

WISDOM FROM A TURTLE

If you stand too close to your reflection, you do not see the full picture of who you are * When one heart speaks, other hearts cannot help but listen * Always keep your mouth closed when cleaning the toilet * Don't stick your neck out too far * Take care of your hardware and it will take care of you * Don't trust people who tell you not to trust anyone * Personality is an art form * Sometimes you have to make sacrifices and you may not like it, but you do it * Try not to be at loggerheads * Leave a little early so you don't have to race to be on time * People are not toys * Avoid posting comments online, period * Swim with a buddy * It's OK to stop hiding, come out of your shell, and be yourself * Nobody wants to be criticized * Forgive freely even though it may be hard to do * Please don't throw out the baby with the bass-water * Love someone for who they are, not what they look like * All that teenage ninja stuff is only in the movies * Be able to laugh at yourself * Realize that others may be in pain and be patient * Hibernate when you need to * Be kind and thankful * Never eat potato salad the picnickers have left behind * Look deeper than the obvious * Keep searching for that higher power and haply ye may find him